The Character of Elsie Dinsmore

MICHAEL DANTE APRILE

CUMBERLAND HOUSE

NASHVILLE, TENNESSEE

The Character of Elsie Dinsmore

CONTENTS

PREFACE

This book was written by members of our family who desire, as Elsie did, to follow the Godly character traits, exemplified by Jesus Christ, in their everyday walk. We felt that Elsie Dinsmore, the character created by Martha Finley in the 1800's, aptly illustrates many of these qualities. Through Elsie's eyes, we have attempted to show how a person whose desire it is to follow the Lord can take up their cross and follow Him.

ACKNOWLEDGEMENTS

Our five children are blessed with many talents. I would like to thank our two daughters, Amy and Elizabeth, who sat diligently for many evenings combing over the drafts of this document to make sure that it revealed Elsie's true nature and speech.

Thanks also to our whole family for their patience and support while we completed this effort.

Special thanks to our good friend, Lee Bereza, who spent endless hours proofreading and fine tuning our book and encouraging us to complete it.

To God be the glory!

The Character of Elsie Dinsmore

INTRODUCTION

The purpose of this book is to reveal to you, the reader, the Christ-like character of Elsie Dinsmore, through her own recollection and according to her portrayal by the author, Martha Finley, who created Elsie on paper for our enrichment. The number of godly character traits that Elsie lives out is exhaustive. A total of thirty-eight character traits were examined while working on this book as they directly related to Elsie's life as a young girl.

A Special Opportunity for Application

It is our hope that readers of this book will gain a first-hand understanding of these character traits so they may apply them to their lives. One way to help your children understand and apply what they have learned through these character building exercises is to have each of them create a CHARACTER BUILDING JOURNAL. Any kind of notebook will do—a spiral notebook, a bound journal, a three-ring binder with notebook paper, a folder, or a black and white composition book. Use what works for your family. At the end of each chapter, there is an application section containing questions and suggestions designed to help your child think about the character qualities Elsie has exhibited and how these same qualities can be exhibited in their own lives. This should not be administered as a test but rather as an opportunity for positive introspection and growth. Have your children revisit their journals from time to time for a character building review. This way they can measure how their character growth is proceeding—like a growth chart.

As we hope you will see, it is possible even today, though it is often a determined struggle, to practice these virtues. May God bless you in your every attempt.

ALERTNESS

*Being aware of that which is taking place around me so that
I have the right response to it.*

Elsie's Alertness Saves the Surprise

I was going through and showing Papa each of the gifts I had
bought people in the family for Christmas. Dear old Mammy was
helping me open the bundles quickly one-by-one and then
bundling them back as Papa acknowledged them. I was being a bit
hasty about opening the bundles but I was also being alert.

"This is a turban for Aunt Phillis, and this is a pound of
tobacco for old Uncle Jack, and a nice pipe, too. Look, mammy!
Won't he be pleased? And here's some flannel for poor, old
Aunt Dinah, who has the rheumatism, and that— Oh! No,
no, mammy! Don't you open that! It's a nice shawl for her, papa,"
I whispered in his ear.

I am glad that I was staying alert, or else Mammy would have
seen her Christmas present and that would have spoiled the surprise for her on Christmas morning. It certainly is not a good idea
to be so excited and wrapped up in the events that are going on
around me that I do not remain alert.

"Stay awake and pray not to be put to the test . . ."
—MARK 14:38, NJB

Other Character Traits Demonstrated

When Elsie saw that Mammy's seeing her Christmas surprise
might steal some well-deserved joy from her, she was able to
demonstrate LOVE. She showed Mammy love by being alert to

3

what she needed and certainly did not expect anything in return. Being alert showed Elsie's love for Mammy, and Elsie became aware that Mammy would enjoy the shawl more as a surprise on Christmas Day than to discover it accidentally.

Elsie spent as much money as she had to be sure that the servants received gifts that they really deserved. By not being stingy with what God had given her and realizing that all she had belonged to Him, she was able to demonstrate true GENEROSITY.

God blessed Elsie with a sensitive spirit that made her especially alert to the spirit and emotions of those who were around her. Her SENSITIVITY caused her to remember that the house servants would each cherish receiving a specially chosen gift from her.

She was never treated as an equal among the rest of the immediate Dinsmore family members. This, however, was not so bad when she considered it gave her greater COMPASSION for the servants in the household. Elsie had come to know that her heavenly Father gave her this position out of His desire to make her more like Jesus.

Purchasing all those gifts while carefully picking out just the right gift and being mindful of each person's needs was how Elsie demonstrated her GRATEFULNESS. Every gift was like a personal thank you to each recipient.

Elsie's Alertness Spares Her

Sometimes alertness served as a memory allowing me to have the right response ready for Papa so that he did not think me forgetful or irresponsible all the time. I recall the instance when Papa sent me to his room to speak with me about something I could tell was not to his liking. The expression on his face showed he was not at all pleased with me, and I thought hard about what the matter could be.

Then I remembered the time that I had sat on the floor when there were plenty of chairs available in the living room. Papa did not approve of this and considered such behavior a very unladylike and slovenly trick.

So, as soon as Papa came in the room, I went up to him, put my hand on his and asked his forgiveness for forgetting his request that I sit on the furniture instead of the floor. Papa seemed to be consoled by my proper response to the exact offense. However, he quickly brought up one more problem.

"I think you disobeyed in another matter," he said.

Being alert to that which he was referring, my immediate response was, "Yes, sir, I know it was very naughty to ask why, but I think I will remember not to do it again. Dear papa, won't you forgive me?"

Being alert to every instance of his objections and being able to respond correctly persuaded Papa to forgive me for the offense and convinced him, as was true, that I was aware of and sorry for my offenses.

Other Character Traits Demonstrated

The way in which Elsie was able to think for herself about each of the offenses she committed against Papa's authority showed Papa she was RESPONSIBLE. In this way, she was able to show responsibility through knowing and doing what her heavenly Father and Papa were expecting from her—without being asked.

Papa could readily see that Elsie was SINCERE. She was eager to do what was right, and Papa perceived that she had pure motives. She always had a sincere desire to please the Lord by doing what was right.

Elsie Uses Alertness in Making a Request

A good many of the little boys and girls were going after strawberries with Miss Allison one afternoon, and I wanted so to go along myself. I knew that I would have to get Papa's approval to go along. He would be back home after my nap, and I planned to ask him then.

When Papa came home, I hurried down to meet him, but he was engaged in conversation with Miss Allison's brother, Edward. Papa acknowledged me with a glance as I entered the room. He reached an arm out to receive me and kept up his conversation with Mr. Allison even while kissing my cheek.

I remained alert with my eyes fixed lovingly upon his face so I would be sure not to miss his slightest acknowledgement that I could make my request. Even Miss Rose noticed how I watched him as they went on about some scientific question with great seriousness.

As soon as Papa paused to speak to me, I quickly, almost without taking a breath, made my request to him so as not to be interrupted until I heard his answer.

Other Character Traits Demonstrated

Had Elsie simply broken into the room where Papa and Mr. Allison were having their conversation and blurted out the question about going strawberry gathering with the children and Mrs. Allison, Papa would have been quite disturbed and displeased with her. That is why she used CAUTIOUSNESS to be sure to make her request when the timing was just right. She had learned that a cautious person can achieve the right reaction by acting at the appropriate time.

"Also, that the soul be without knowledge, it is not good; and he that hasteth with his feet sinneth."

—PROVERBS 19:2

Elsie could have required Papa to give her his immediate attention for a question she thought needed his urgent attention, but she chose to demonstrate DEFERENCE. She knew that she possessed the freedom to speak when she needed to, but she chose to limit her freedom, so that she could not possibly offend or upset others around her. This is the way Jesus would have her behave, as she knew He would prefer to serve others before being served. To break in on Papa's conversation would have been rude.

"It is good neither to eat flesh, nor to drink wine, nor any thing whereby thy brother stumbleth, or is offended, or is made weak."

—ROMANS 14:21

Character Building Journal

1. In this chapter, you can see how Elsie learned about or applied the positive character trait of ALERTNESS. In what areas of your life could you put this good character quality into practice? List some ideas in your Journal.

2. In what ways have you exemplified or shown to others this character quality? List them in your Journal.

3. Are there areas of your life that could use a little improvement with regard to ALERTNESS? List those in your Journal as well and talk with your parents about ways for you to improve in this area.

ATTENTIVENESS

*Showing the worth of a person by giving undivided attention
to his words and emotions.*

Elsie Is Attentive to Arthur

I had been in the schoolroom by myself for about half an hour
when I heard the door open. It was Arthur. I must confess that I
was not pleased to see him. I was trying to work out my examples
and Arthur had a habit of teasing and tormenting me so I could not
accomplish anything.

However, Arthur seemed to be acting different than usual. He
sat right down at his desk and leaned his head upon his hand in an
attitude of dejection.

Wondering what ailed him, I asked, "What is the matter, Arthur?"

"Nothing much," he said, gruffly, and he turned his back to me.

By giving my undivided attention to Arthur, I accomplished
two things that day. I was able to tell Arthur, without really saying
so, that I cared about him and how he was feeling. And, being
attentive, I was able to tell that Arthur did not want to be confronted at that moment. In these two ways, I showed Arthur that
his feelings were important and had worth to me.

*"We ought, then, to turn our minds more attentively than before to
what we have been taught, so that we do not drift away."*
—HEBREWS 2:1, NJB

Related Character Trait

When Arthur was feeling dejected, Elsie was able to respond
to his needs correctly by staying ALERT. ALERTNESS comes from

being aware of that which is taking place around you so that you can have the right response to it.

"Stay awake and pray not to be put to the test. The spirit is willing enough but human nature is weak."
—MARK 14:38, NJB

Character Building Journal

1.   In this chapter, you can see how Elsie learned about or applied the positive character trait of ATTENTIVENESS. In what areas of your life could you put this good character quality into practice? List some ideas in your Journal.

2.   In what ways have you exemplified or shown to others this character quality? List them in your Journal.

3.   Are there areas of your life that could use a little improvement with regard to ATTENTIVENESS? List those in your Journal as well and talk with your parents about ways for you to improve in this area.

AVAILABILITY

Making my own schedule and priorities secondary to the wishes of those I am serving.

Elsie Is Available for Mammy

I love dear Mammy and the things she does for me. She has always been there for me and been like a mamma to me. I desired to help her whenever possible and tried to be available for her in what little ways I could.

One evening, while Mammy was combing back her hair and getting ready for bed, I quickly said my prayers and went to the table beside her bed to read to her from the Bible.

I know she appreciated that I was able to be available for her. She and I shared a deep love for the Bible stories.

I could have gone straight to my bed and waited for Mammy to wait hand-and-foot on me. After all, that was her duty. However, I chose to make my own schedule and priorities secondary to my heavenly Father's that night, by serving Mammy.

"There is nobody else that I can send who is like him and cares sincerely for your well-being; they all want to work for themselves and not for Jesus Christ."
—PHILIPPIANS 2:20-21, NJB

Related Character Trait

Elsie was so glad that God brought Mammy into her life and she was anxious to show her HOSPITALITY. She cheerfully shared some spiritual refreshment with Mammy and with many others who were less appreciative.

Elsie Is Available for Aunt Lora

One day, while we were on a carriage ride, the horses took fright and went to a full gallop. This threatened at every turn to upset the carriage. A brave man managed to stop them, at the risk of his own life.

All were silent as we walked the little distance to the house. Aunt Lora looked pale, and more grave and thoughtful than I had ever seen her.

Upon seeing that I was not shaken by the whole event, Lora expressed her desire to be a Christian like me.

"Elsie, if you could only tell me how to be a Christian," she said. "I mean now to try very hard; indeed, I am determined never to rest until I am one."

It was at this time that my heart filled with joy for her. I immediately told her that, "Every one that asketh, receiveth; and he that seeketh, findeth; and to him that knocketh, it shall be opened." I then shared several other verses with her, answering all her questions by referring to the Bible.

Other Character Traits Demonstrated

Elsie's heartfelt joy for Aunt Lora's decision to come to the Savior demonstrated ENTHUSIASM. She was just expressing with her spirit the joy of her soul for Lora's soul. Aunt Lora's sudden decision surprised Elsie so that she could not help being excited and astounded, all at once.

Elsie was mostly perceptive about Aunt Lora's need to understand the answers to some objections she had held in her breast about salvation. She was able to exercise her SENSITIVITY for this purpose, by finding the appropriate passage from scripture to fit the questions. She pointed to each passage as she read it to allow Aunt Lora to see that she was quoting it correctly.

By addressing Aunt Lora's questions from the way the Lord would see them, Elsie was able to call on His WISDOM to speak the right words to meet her needs. This ability helped her to lead Aunt Lora along the path to salvation.

Character Building Journal

1.   In this chapter, you can see how Elsie learned about or applied the positive character trait of AVAILABILITY. In what areas of your life could you put this good character quality into practice? List some ideas in your Journal.

2.   In what ways have you exemplified or shown to others this character quality? List them in your Journal.

3.   Are there areas of your life that could use a little improvement with regard to AVAILABILITY? List those in your Journal as well and talk with your parents about ways for you to improve in this area.

BOLDNESS

Confidence that what I have to say or do is true and right and just in the sight of God.

Elsie Exhibits Boldness with Papa

At one point in my life Papa became very ill, and I had it in my heart to comfort him in any way that I could. I made a special effort to stay by his side and do whatever I could to make him comfortable. At some points, Papa had to command that I go down to eat meals.

I knew that my main comfort came from reading the Scriptures and expected that this would be a comfort to Papa as well. However, when I started to read Papa passages from the Bible, he grew weary of them and requested that I read from another book, full of fiction and worldly deeds.

Though I pleaded with Papa, he insisted sternly that I read the other book to him. The reason I did not want to read that book was that it was the Sabbath. I had been taught, and I firmly believed that it was not right to read such things on the Sabbath, but Papa took my objection as willful disobedience. From that point on, as punishment, Papa forbade me from visiting him.

My sorrow from not being able to be with him and do things for him was great. He forbade me to see him until I admitted I was wrong to think I could not read such worldly fiction on the Sabbath.

Though I struggled against my earnest feelings of love for Papa and wanted his greatest affection for me, I knew that when it came to breaking the Sabbath, I must stand firm. A mighty struggle was going on in my heart, and it was very hard for me to give up my Papa's love. But the love of Jesus—ah, that was even more precious!

So, I went to him and said with tremulous and emotional tones in my voice, "Papa, dear, dear Papa. I do love you so very, very much, and I do want to be to you a good, obedient child. But, Papa, Jesus says, 'He that loveth father or mother more than me, is not worthy of me,' and I must love Jesus best and keep His commandments always. But you bid me say that I am sorry I refuse to break them and that I will yield implicit obedience to you, even though you should command me to disobey him. Oh, Papa, I cannot do that, even though you should never love me again—even though you should put me to death."

I cannot say that Papa was pleased with my little speech, but I had to be bold about the principle that my heavenly Father laid out in scripture. In this instance, I was confident that what I had to say was right and just in the sight of my heavenly Father.

"And now, Lord, behold their threatenings: and grant unto thy servants, that with all boldness they may speak thy word . . ."
—ACTS 4:29

Related Character Trait

Confronting Papa in this way was most difficult for Elsie, because she so desired and needed his love and acceptance. She knew that it would require a cross to give up her personal rights and expectations to her heavenly Father in MEEKNESS so that she could be bold and speak the truth in this instance.

"My soul, wait thou only upon God; for my expectation is from him."
—PSALM 62:5

14

Elsie Shows Boldness with Arthur

Then there was the time when I thought I would be frightened to death. Arthur saw the gold chain of grandpa's watch, which had been laid on a table. Arthur was so tempted by its sparkle he snatched it up and ran off with it.

While playing with the watch, Arthur dropped it. The crystal broke, and the back was dented. When Arthur picked it up, it had stopped running. Arthur, becoming scared and defensive, said to me, "I'll tell you what, if any of you dare to tell of me, I'll make you sorry for it to the last day of your life. Do you hear?"

When I discovered that Arthur planned to set the blame on Jim, if questioned, I immediately confronted him.

"Arthur, grandpa will know that someone did it, and surely you would not wish that an innocent person get punished for your fault."

"I don't care who gets punished, just so Papa does not find out that I did it," he answered furiously. "If you dare to tell on me, I'll pay you for it."

I knew that I must speak the truth for Jesus' sake, and I confronted Arthur once more.

"I shall say nothing, unless it becomes necessary to save the innocent, or I am forced to speak. In that case, I shall tell the truth," I said firmly.

I remember Arthur was not pleased with my statement and tried to hit me with his fist; however, I ducked behind a tree and then ran for my life.

Elsie Shows Boldness in Principle

Arthur was always up to something, and I can't claim that it was always something good. This time was no different as he approached me to loan him some money. He told me that he knew

I had a generous allowance and that he needed to borrow some of it.

When I questioned him about the purpose for borrowing the money, Arthur replied, in defense, that it was none of my business. When I explained that Papa would not be pleased and think of it as disobedient of me if I lent money to him for something wrong, Arthur objected by saying that I pick and choose when to be obedient.

I told him I would not do a thing when I knew that it would break God's command. Understanding the principle behind what I told him, Arthur admitted that he had been gambling several weeks earlier and owed Dick Percival a dollar or so. After gambling and losing again to him last night, Arthur was in real danger of being reported to his papa.

That is when I told him frankly, "Oh! Arthur, you've been gambling. How could you do so? It is very wicked! You'll go to ruin, Arthur, if you keep on in such bad ways. Do go to grandpa and tell him all about it and promise never to do so again, and I am sure he will forgive you and pay your debts. Then you will feel a great deal happier."

Arthur was not pleased with my advice. After he tried to threaten me and then tried to talk me into falsely writing in my expense book that I used the money for another purpose, I told him, "Arthur, I could never do such a wicked thing! I would not deceive Papa so for any money, and even if I did, he would be sure to find it out."

Although I did not tell on Arthur, I was glad that I held fast to my principles with boldness.

Elsie Shows Boldness in Witness

I often prayed for Papa that he would come to know Jesus as his Savior, but rarely did I get the opportunity to talk with him about it. So, when I came to him and said my prayers in his presence one evening, as usual, I included him in them.

Papa asked me if I had said some prayers for him and what did I say, so I was obliged to tell him and spoke with uncertain boldness, "I asked, as I always do, that you might love Jesus, papa, and be very happy, indeed, both in this world and the next."

"Thank you," Papa said, "but why are you so anxious that I should love him? It would not trouble me if you did not, so long as you loved and obeyed me."

This made me want to cry, but I knew that this was an opportunity that I must not let pass by, and with a tremulous voice I replied, "Because I know, Papa, that no one can go to heaven who does not love Jesus, nor ever be really happy anywhere, for the Bible says so. Papa, you always punish me when I am disobedient to you, and the Bible says that God is our Father and will punish us if we do not obey him. One of his commandments is: 'Thou shalt love the Lord thy God.' In another place, it says: 'Every one that loveth Him that begat Him also is begotten of Him.'"

"Seeing then that we have such hope, we use great plainness of speech . . ."
—2 CORINTHIANS 3:12, NJB

Related Character Trait

Elsie had a real task to speak the truth with boldness to Papa, which required that she use PERSUASIVENESS to guide the truth around what Papa had already determined to be the way things must be. Her love for Papa and her love for the truth made it possible for her to recall the appropriate scripture that made this possible. Even though Papa tried not to show it, she was sure that her words touched his heart that evening.

*"And the servant of the Lord must not strive; but be gentle
unto all men, apt to teach, patient . . ."*

—2 TIMOTHY 2:24, NJB

Character Building Journal

1.   In this chapter, you can see how Elsie learned about or applied the positive character trait of BOLDNESS. In what areas of your life could you put this good character quality into practice? List some ideas in your Journal.

2.   In what ways have you exemplified or shown to others this character quality? List them in your Journal.

3.   Are there areas of your life that could use a little improvement with regard to BOLDNESS? List those in your Journal as well and talk with your parents about ways for you to improve in this area.

CAUTIOUSNESS

Knowing how important right timing is in accomplishing right actions.

Elsie Is Cautious with Enna

I knew there was going to be a problem as soon as Enna entered the room. I had spent nearly all my spare time knitting a purse for dear Miss Rose Allison to give to her when she left for home. I was sure that the purse would be special to Miss Allison, since I made it with my own hands.

As soon as I realized that the opening of the door was Enna entering, I hastily attempted to conceal the purse by thrusting it into my pocket, but it was too late, for Enna had seen it and demanded it from me.

Enna immediately threatened to tell her mamma if I did not give the purse to her that I made for Miss Allison. I tried to be cautious with her by offering to let her hold it for just a few minutes, if she agreed not to soil it. I was careful to speak with a gentle tone and offered to get some more silk and beads to make her one just like it. I even explained that this particular purse was for Miss Allison who was leaving the next morning and that I would not have time to make another before she left.

I was horrified, but not surprised, that Enna did not accept my offer. She demanded *that* one to keep. She even attempted to snatch the purse right out of my hand, before it was completed.

Cautiously, I held the purse up out of her reach, and she eventually gave up trying to reach it and stormed out of the room crying and screaming with a convincing passion.

I realized then that I would be made to give up the purse and determined that had I been more cautious, I would never have allowed Enna to see the purse in the first place — out of site, out of mind as Mammy would say.

"The thoughts of the diligent tend only to plenteousness; but of every one that is hasty only to want."

—PROVERBS 21:5

Other Character Traits Demonstrated

With children like Enna and others her age, there is no persuading short of bribery, yet bribery should be out of the question as a sin against our heavenly Father and his commandments. PERSUASIVENESS comes from caring about the outcome for the person you are trying to convince more than the outcome for us. If a person is wrong about something, it is because they do not know the truth or their truth is not based on what the Bible tells us. Once a person has established something that is false as the truth, in their mind, those false ideas become roadblocks and sometimes stumbling blocks. The best way to avoid a contest, as Elsie soon had with Enna for the purse, is to help them avoid obstacles on the way to the truth.

"In meekness instructing those that oppose themselves; if God peradventure will give them repentance to the acknowledging of the truth."

—2 TIMOTHY 2:25

Elsie wished she could have been more like Jesus, as she attempted to persuade Enna to give up the idea of the purse she had made for Miss Allison. She could see later that she probably could have used a bit more DISCRETION. The important thing, in a situation like that, is to avoid any words, actions, or attitudes that would cause Enna to go off crying to her Mamma. Maybe her Mamma was right about the idea that "You will not give it to her" instead of what Elsie said which was "I cannot give it to her." She probably should have offered Enna the purse. Maybe she would have turned it down or grown tired of it quickly.

"A prudent man foreseeth the evil, and hideth himself: but the simple pass on, and are punished."
—PROVERBS 22:3

Character Building Journal

1. In this chapter, you can see how Elsie learned about or applied the positive character trait of CAUTIOUSNESS. In what areas of your life could you put this good character quality into practice? List some ideas in your Journal.

2. In what ways have you exemplified or shown to others this character quality? List them in your Journal.

3. Are there areas of your life that could use a little improvement with regard to CAUTIOUSNESS? List those in your Journal as well and talk with your parents about ways for you to improve in this area.

COMPASSION

Investing whatever is necessary to heal the hurts of others.

Elsie Shows Compassion to Arthur

After all the horrible things that Arthur did to torment me, I still felt some compassion for him when I heard his deep sigh from out on the veranda. I rose and went to him. Seeing that he looked quite dejected, I went over and placed my hand gently upon his shoulder.

"What ails you, Arthur? Can I do anything for you? I will be very glad if I can."

At first, Arthur did not want to admit that I could help, but then he admitted I could. He thought I would rather do something to get back at him than to help him and was amazed to find out differently.

I explained to him that none of those things he had done mattered to me now. I had discovered, I admitted, that it was a rather good thing that I did not get to go for a ride, because I got to go out later with Aunt Adelaide and Miss Allison. That was more to my liking. Then I encouraged him to tell me what he wanted.

"But whoso hath this world's good, and seeth his brother have need,
and shutteth up his bowels of compassion from him,
how dwelleth the love of God in him?"

—1 JOHN 3:17

Other Character Traits Demonstrated

The Lord gave Elsie a special SENSITIVITY to people who were hurting, and perhaps that was why she was so sensitive and allowed things to hurt her so easily. When she heard Arthur's large sigh from the veranda and then saw his head bent down with his eyes fixed on the floor, it touched her sensitive heart. Even before that moment, she had wanted to figure out how she could return good for evil.

"Rejoice with them that do rejoice, and weep with them that weep."
—ROMANS 12:15

It is difficult for a young girl like Elsie not to have a spurt of selfishness, every now and then. However, her desire was to be like Jesus, and He is the opposite of selfishness, which is LOVE. The Bible says that God is love and this means that Jesus is like his Father. Elsie also desired to be like her Father. The real question for her was what would Jesus do with Arthur in this situation. She knew the answer and believed He would provide for Arthur's needs and not expect any reward for it. This is why she chose to show love to Arthur, instead of being selfish about the way he treated her.

"And though I bestow all my goods to feed the poor, and though I give my body to be burned, and have not charity, it profiteth me nothing."
—1 CORINTHIANS 13:3

Elsie could have retaliated for the way Arthur treated her by acting like she did not care about him when he wanted to ask her a favor. Instead, she made up her mind to show GENEROSITY by giving the time the Lord gave to her to work on her drawings to him and his needs. She knew that this was using what belongs to God to serve her heavenly Father.

The Character of Elsie Dinsmore

"But this I say, He which soweth sparingly shall reap also
sparingly; and he which soweth bountifully
shall reap also bountifully."

—2 CORINTHIANS 9:6

When Arthur tried to ask Elsie for something he needed, he did not feel free to ask her because he did not feel he had received FORGIVENESS. There are stories in the Bible that show us how we put people in "jail" when we do not forgive them. As soon as she told Arthur, "Oh! never mind" and that she did not care anymore about the things he did, he opened up and told her everything like a bird released from its cage.

"And be ye kind one to another, tenderhearted, forgiving one another,
even as God for Christ's sake hath forgiven you."

—EPHESIANS 4:32

Elsie Shows Compassion for a Bird

When I saw a tiny hummingbird trapped under a glass vase struggling to escape, I felt sure that it was something Arthur must have done. Being the tenderhearted person I am, I could not stand to see any living creature suffer so.

I had compassion for the little bird and, lifting the glass, I let it go free. I was not aware until a short time later that Papa had captured the little creature, rare as it turned out to be, for his collection.

I still feel that it was cruel to hold such a little thing captive in such a confined space and felt like I might have done the correct thing to follow my sense of compassion.

"And one of you say unto them, Depart in peace, be ye warmed
and filled; notwithstanding ye give them not those things

24

which are needful to the body; what doth it profit?"
—JAMES 2:16

Other Character Traits Demonstrated

Elsie had a keen SENSITIVITY to suffering creatures here on this earth. This must have been what made her react with a strong desire to release the little prisoner. Without waiting, she raised the vase, and the bird was gone.

"For I was an hungred, and ye gave me meat: I was thirsty, and ye gave me drink: I was a stranger, and ye took me in."
—MATTHEW 25:35

Elsie Shows Compassion to Papa

When Papa became ill with a bad headache, he told me I was "as nice a little nurse as anybody need ask for." He told me that I knew just the right thing to do for him. I remember telling him that I suffered from headaches so often that I had found out what one wants at such times.

I enjoyed being permitted to stay with Papa and took advantage of this time to bathe his head with my hands, smooth his hair, shake up his pillows, give him his medicines, fan him, and read or sing to him in soft, sweet tones.

Other Character Traits Demonstrated

Elsie's ATTENTIVENESS was apparent when, after her morning lessons, she noticed Papa lying on the sofa in his room looking flushed and feverish.

She was able to show DILIGENCE by remaining at her Papa's side, except when he forbade her to be there and had to insist that she go down to eat or go out to get some fresh air and exercise.

"And whatsoever ye do, do it heartily, as to the Lord,
and not unto men."
—COLOSSIANS 3:23

In caring for her Papa, Elsie used GENTLENESS by stroking his hair and bathing his head with her cool hands.

"But we were gentle among you, even as a nurse
cherisheth her children."
—1 THESSALONIANS 2:7

Elsie whole-heartedly gave herself in LOVE to her Papa, and her desire was to see him well again.

Elsie Shows Compassion to Adelaide

When my Aunt Adelaide lost someone dear to her, I was able to put aside my own sorrows to join with her in her bereavement. I realized that Adelaide, not knowing my Lord, would not have the same consolation I did in being able to carry my sorrows to him.

To Adelaide, all was darkness and sorrow. If only she had the compassion of the Savior, who promised to love her and never to leave or forsake her.

I showed my sympathy in various little kind offices: sitting for hours beside her couch, gently fanning her, handing her a drink of cold water, bringing her sweet-scented flowers, and anticipating every want.

I took this opportunity to tell her about how Jesus was able to comfort her if only she would go to Him. He loved her so deeply that He died to save her.

"Rejoice with them that do rejoice, and weep with them that weep."
—ROMANS 12:15

Other Character Traits Demonstrated

Through her God-given SENSITIVITY, Elsie sensed that it was important to join with her Aunt Adelaide in her grief. She needed someone much more than Elsie did with whom to share her sorrow. Elsie, after all, had a compassionate Savior.

Elsie's ability to show GENTLENESS greatly helped her Aunt Adelaide in her time of bereavement. She saw everything during that time as darkness and despair.

"To the weak became I as weak, that I might gain the weak: I am made all things to all men, that I might by all means save some."
—1 CORINTHIANS 9:22

Elsie Shows More Compassion for Adelaide

When I found Aunt Adelaide upon her couch in her room, face down in her pillows, sobbing violently, my own eyes filled with tears. I carefully approached her and attempted to sooth her grief with words of gentle, loving sympathy.

I told her in a tremulous voice that I could understand how she felt, because I have experienced some sorrow. The one I wanted to be with me couldn't be there. I was thinking of how I wanted my mother's love and had pined all of my life for a mother's love. Then, Papa had sent Mammy away as a punishment for me.

Character Building Journal

1. In this chapter, you can see how Elsie learned about or applied the positive character trait of COMPASSION. In what areas of your life could you put this good character quality into practice? List some ideas in your Journal.

2. In what ways have you exemplified or shown to others this character quality? List them in your Journal.

3. Are there areas of your life that could use a little improvement with regard to COMPASSION? List those in your Journal as well and talk with your parents about ways for you to improve in this area.

Contentment

*Realizing God has provided everything that I need
for my present happiness.*

Elsie Finds Contentment through Christ

When Miss Allison left, I found myself quite alone again. I became very sorrowful and looked inwardly to examine my sins and myself. For, I knew that they, at least in my mind, were many.

I soon had begun to recount and confess my sins and sorrows in the ears of the dear Savior whom I love so well. I told him that when I had suffered for what I did well, I had not taken it patiently, and I earnestly pleaded that I might be made like unto the meek and lowly Jesus.

As I sobbed in bursts of tears, they fell on the pages of my little Bible. But when I was finished praying and when I rose from my knees, a wonderful thing happened. The burden of sin and sorrow was all gone, and my heart was suddenly light and happy with a sweet sense of peace that I had been pardoned.

Once again, as before, I was made to experience the blessing of my heavenly Father's forgiveness.

*"If we confess our sins, he is faithful and just to forgive us our sins,
and to cleanse us from all unrighteousness."*

—1 John 1:9

Another Character Trait Demonstrated

Elsie's spirit immediately revealed her JOYFULNESS as she turned from what can only be described as sorrow and perhaps self-pity. She knew at once that her soul had entered into fellowship with her heavenly Father and that He forgave her for her sins.

"Thou wilt shew me the path of life: in thy presence is fullness of joy; at thy right hand there are pleasures for evermore."

—PSALM 16:11

Elsie Finds Contentment in Stewed Fruit

I thought I was going to receive quite a treat at breakfast with Papa when Pomp served me a delicious-looking hot buttered roll. As I began to savor the smell of the bread and watched the butter melt before my eyes, Papa told Pomp that I was not to eat hot bread and should be allowed to eat only the cold.

Pomp then began to set up a cup by my plate for coffee, which is one thing that I like very much. Suddenly Papa instructed Pomp to remove the coffee.

"Take that away, Pomp, and bring Miss Elsie a tumbler of milk. Or would you prefer water, Elsie?"

I replied that I preferred milk, but I actually preferred coffee, which I was extremely fond of, and it was something of a trial to give it up.

Then Papa put a spoonful of stewed fruit on my plate and, placing his hand briefly on my head, said he intended to keep me away from butter and other bad things until I was at least ten or eleven years old. He said he planned to take good care of me.

I was so pleased at his caress and word of encouragement that I ate the cold bread without butter and the stewed fruit and drank the glass of milk with a happy heart. Soon this breakfast menu continued without the caresses and encouragement, and I often looked with longing eyes at the hot buttered rolls and coffee that others were eating. However, I contented myself by thinking that Papa knew what was best and that I ought to be content with whatever he gives me.

"And having food and raiment let us be therewith content."
—1 TIMOTHY 6:8

Elsie Finds Contentment in the Lord Being with Her

After a rather horrific carriage ride, when the horses were spooked and went immediately to a full gallop, Aunt Lora was very pale, but I went to my Bible to read. The Lord gave me the verse: "Yea, though I walk through the valley of the shadow of death, I will fear no evil; for thou art with me."

I told Aunt Lora how it made me so happy to think that Jesus was there with me, and that if I were killed, I should only fall asleep to wake up again in His arms. I went on to ask her rhetorically, "Then how could I be afraid?"

"He that dwelleth in the secret place of the most High shall abide under the shadow of the Almighty."
—PSALM 91:1

Other Character Traits Demonstrated

Elsie was able to feel secure around Papa and among the household servants, such as Mammy. However, she still felt her greatest SECURITY from her heavenly Father who seemed to always be there with her. Even in her deepest sorrow, when she was alone and when all seemed against her, He was there.

*". . . be content with such things as ye have: for he hath said, I will
never leave thee, nor forsake thee."*

—HEBREWS 13:5

When Elsie was dealing with the prospect of losing her life or
Aunt Lora's to a terrible carriage accident, she needed a special
WISDOM that could come from no one but her heavenly Father. At
these times she was content to turn to special passages in scripture
for what she needed.

*"The secret of the LORD is with them that fear him; and he will
shew them his covenant."*

—PSALM 25:14

Elsie needed only, in her FAITH, to visualize what her
heavenly Father intended to do in a situation and then to behave
in complete surrendered harmony with that decision. The Lord
gave her the strength to be content in this.

"For we walk by faith, not by sight."

—2 CORINTHIANS 5:7

Elsie Explains Her Contentment to Papa

Not too long ago, I had one of those rare opportunities to talk
to Papa about Mamma. He explained that he did not know her
that long before she went on to be with Jesus in heaven.

I told Papa that I longed to see her again and was joyful that,
since she loved the Lord, I would see her soon in Heaven. After I
asked Papa if he loved Jesus, he asked me without answering,
"Do you, Elsie?"

Hoping that he would understand my meaning, I told Papa that I loved Jesus more than I loved him or anyone else. Papa wondered how I knew such a thing. I was surprised by this question and replied to him, "Just as I know I love you, Papa."

I told Papa how I loved to talk of Jesus, to tell Him all my troubles, and to ask Him to forgive my sins and make me holy. I told him how it is so sweet to know that He loves me and will always love me, even if no one else does.

A Related Character Trait

The VIRTUE that the Lord gave to Elsie comes from obedience to His Word. She strove to follow the way He taught her as He worked in her life to make her holy. Some people have observed that her spirit is different than others. Her desire was to be pure in her Savior.

"And beside this, giving all diligence, add to your faith virtue; and to virtue knowledge."

—2 PETER 1:5

Elsie Shows Her Contentment to Papa

At a time when I played late in the nursery with the other children and enjoyed it so, my Papa entered the room comparing the clock on the wall with his watch. He asked immediately why I was still not in bed at such a late hour. Everyone objected, asking whether I could stay another hour, but Papa said that I must go right away.

Being obedient, as I always tried to be, I got up and went straight away. However, this did not at all make me sad. I was very happy to obey my Papa and to leave the merry group at once.

Papa was very pleased to see my cheerful and obedient response to his command and called me his good, obedient, little girl. I told him how much I loved him, and that I loved him all the more for not letting me have my own way but always making me obey the rules. I felt content in this because I realized it was training me to be like Jesus.

"O that thou hadst hearkened to my commandments! then had thy peace been as a river, and thy righteousness as the waves of the sea."

—ISAIAH 48:18

Other Character Traits Demonstrated

Despite the annoyance of being forced by Papa to leave the merry group that was in the nursery, Elsie was content to go at once. The LOYALTY that she had for her father matched the loyalty that she had for her heavenly Father.

"Hereby perceive we the love of God, because he laid down his life for us: and we ought to lay down our lives for the brethren."

—1 JOHN 3:16

Knowing that Jesus was in complete OBEDIENCE to His father on earth, which made Him obedient also to His Father in Heaven, Elsie was content to do exactly as Papa required. Going straight to bed when Papa commanded her to showed her obedience to her heavenly Father.

"Children, obey your parents in all things: for this is well pleasing unto the Lord."

—COLOSSIANS 3:20

Being ready to go straight to bed as Papa commanded allowed Elsie to show her GRATEFULNESS to him for permitting her to play in the nursery for the time that he did. She wanted him to know that she appreciated that privilege.

"For who maketh thee to differ from another? and what hast thou that thou didst not receive? now if thou didst receive it, why dost thou glory, as if thou hadst not received it?"
—1 CORINTHIANS 4:7

Elsie's Papa brought some HUMILITY into her life by forcing her to do what she was told and to be content with it. She thought she would have grown to be prideful if he allowed her to do whatever she wanted and if she never had to obey the rules.

"Likewise, ye younger, submit yourselves unto the elder. Yea, all of you be subject one to another, and be clothed with humility: for God resisteth the proud, and giveth grace to the humble."
—1 PETER 5:5

Elsie's Papa told her how proud he was of her for being an obedient daughter, while giving her a big hug. He was pleased with her DEPENDABILITY when it came to doing what he asked.

"In whose eyes a vile person is contemned; but he honoureth them that fear the LORD. He that sweareth to his own hurt, and changeth not."
—PSALM 15:4

Elsie's Contentment Is in Suffering for Christ

The time my Papa decided to leave me, because I held fast to my faith that what Jesus commanded was first even over what he commanded of me, was one of the deepest sorrows of my young life. It also brought other sorrows as he tried to get me to change my mind and give up the "willful notion," as he often called it.

I knew this was true obedience, but Papa thought of it as disobedience. At the beginning, I looked at all this as suffering that I was not due and could not bear the pain that it brought me. One of the punishments that Papa gave was to separate Mammy from me. My heart was broken by the whole affair. Mammy was very dear to me.

One day, I had a visit from Mrs. Travilla. She brought some things to my attention that I had not considered for some time. As I turned over the leaves of my Bible, I came across the words: "Unto you it is given in the behalf of Christ, not only to believe in him, but also to suffer for his sake."

I rejoiced at the thought that I could be suffering for His sake. To suffer for him was a great privilege. I realized my suffering was because I loved Jesus too much to disobey His commandments, even to please my dear Papa. For this, I was deprived of one privilege, then one comfort after another, and I was subjected to trials that wrung my very heart.

Finally, in this matter, it contented me to remember the verse: "If we suffer, we shall also reign with him." This all brought new joy to my heart.

"But godliness with contentment is great gain."

—1 TIMOTHY 6:6

Other Character Traits

For a little while, with the help of Mrs. Travilla, Elsie seemed to be lent God's very own WISDOM to be able to see how she was doing His will in being willing to suffer for Christ sake. This special knowledge was provided by the Lord that she might find the joy that He was providing her through His grace. Somehow, she just knew He was showing her His approval for suffering.

"The first principle of wisdom is the fear of the Lord, what God's holy ones know—this is understanding."
—PROVERBS 9:10, NJB

In complete FAITH that Elsie had discovered why the Lord allowed her suffering, she began to place her trust in Him. Tears of joy and thankfulness began to fall from her eyes. Almost in an instant, she felt a calm and was peaceful. She actually felt happy, for a time, in the midst of all her sorrow.

"Only faith can guarantee the blessings that we hope for, or prove the existence of the realities that are unseen."
—HEBREWS 11:1, NJB

Elsie Chooses to Show Contentment

When Papa's response was "no" to my request to join Miss Rose and the children in gathering strawberries, I tried in vain to hold back the tears. I had already set my heart on going, which is something I should not have been so foolish to do.

Papa was not pleased with my tearful reaction to his decision and saw it as defiance. He bade me go to his room "until I could be cheerful and pleasant."

Once in his room, I let the tears flow freely. I wiped the tears from my eyes and thought, "what a silly girl I am." I realized that I was crying because I could not have my own way. I knew that this had never before altered Papa's determination in the least. His way, I have usually discovered, is the best in the end.

I thought how I must have disgraced myself before Miss Rose, her mother, and the rest and vexed Papa. Papa said that I could join them when I could be cheerful and pleasant, and, since I thought now I could, that is what I did. Just then, the tea-bell rang, and I went down to join them.

Papa assisted in drawing my chair to the table and, as he did, I lifted my eyes to his face. The look I gave was one that asked forgiveness, and his smile said to me that he forgave me. This gave me a peace and contentment that I showed at once through a big smile.

"Not that I speak in respect of want: for I have learned, in whatsoever state I am, therewith to be content."
—PHILIPPIANS 4:11

Other Character Traits Demonstrated

It was not very long after Elsie was sent to Papa's room that the Lord prompted her SELF-CONTROL and helped her realize that she could be pleasant and cheerful when she was told something she did not want to hear.

"And they that are Christ's have crucified the flesh with the affections and lusts."
—GALATIANS 5:24

The fact that Elsie did not speak to Papa as they sat down to have tea after the incident but instead gave him a non-verbal indication of her desire for reconciliation showed that she had learned DISCRETION. Papa had discretion also as he replied non-verbally. Words sometimes get in the way of truly expressing how we feel.

"The prudent man foreseeth the evil and hideth himself . . ."
—PROVERBS 27:12

Character Building Journal

1. In this chapter, you can see how Elsie learned about or applied the positive character trait of CONTENTMENT. In what areas of your life could you put this good character quality into practice? List some ideas in your Journal.

2. In what ways have you exemplified or shown to others this character quality? List them in your Journal.

3. Are there areas of your life that could use a little improvement with regard to CONTENTMENT? List those in your Journal as well and talk with your parents about ways for you to improve in this area.

CREATIVITY

Approaching a need, a task, or an idea from a new perspective.

Elsie Shows Creativity to Surprise Arthur

One time Arthur asked me to lend him money to buy a beautiful little ship he wanted. I thought it might be a great surprise for him if I didn't give him the money but pretended to just be thinking about it. I told him it was a great deal of money to lend, and that I would give him my answer tomorrow.

My real intention was to go to Pomp and ask him to go buy the vessel for Arthur without him knowing. Arthur thought I was just being stingy. I felt like the surprise would do him some good, as dejected as he was feeling.

I realized that Pomp would have to go out of his way to make the effort for this secret mission to turn out right, so I told him to keep a half a dollar out of the money for his trouble. He was very pleased that I offered the money to him.

Another idea I had was to have Mammy place the ship on Arthur's desk in the schoolroom before he entered there that morning. I even wrote a little note telling him the ship was a gift, so that there would be no misunderstanding.

Other Character Traits Demonstrated

Elsie desired to show her GENEROSITY to Arthur because she really wanted to return good for evil, but also because she knew that the money that she had was really not hers but the Lord's.

"But who am I, and what is my people, that we should be able to offer so willingly after this sort? for all things come of thee, and of thine own have we given thee."

—1 CHRONICLES 29:14

Elsie took care not to be offensive to Arthur or Pomp while putting together the surprise for Arthur. She tried her best to show GENTLENESS as to meet everyone's needs in this kind deed.

"To the weak became I as weak, that I might gain the weak: I am made all things to all men, that I may by all means save some."

—1 CORINTHIANS 9:22

Character Building Journal

1.   In this chapter, you can see how Elsie learned about or applied the positive character trait of CREATIVITY. In what areas of your life could you put this good character quality into practice? List some ideas in your Journal.

2.   In what ways have you exemplified or shown to others this character quality? List them in your Journal.

3.   Are there areas of your life that could use a little improvement with regard to CREATIVITY? List those in your Journal as well and talk with your parents about ways for you to improve in this area.

DECISIVENESS

*The ability to finalize difficult decisions based
on the will and ways of God.*

Elsie Shows Decisiveness in Life Decisions

There came a time in my life that I had to decide between two
equally important matters. It was not an easy decision, and it tore
at my heart. Papa was forcing me to choose between that which
my heart so yearned for—a home with him—which, if I chose, I
would have to take as my rule of faith and practice, not God's Holy
Word, which had hitherto been my guide-book, but Papa's wishes
and commands, which I well knew would sometimes be entirely
opposed to the Lord's teaching.

When I thought over the choice, as difficult as it was, I knew
I had a duty to follow the scriptural passage: "This is the way, walk
ye in it." It seemed like I could hear a voice say, "We ought to obey
God rather than men." To do the other, to me, seemed to be a
wicked sin against my heavenly Father. It was, indeed, an awful
thing to cause my earthly father displeasure, but how much more
horrible would it be to displease my heavenly Father.

There was another difficulty in the decision. If I insisted on
following the ways of the Lord, I would have to attend a boarding
school full of trials and temptations, which I was not quite sure I
could endure. I wished desperately that Papa would spare me
this trial and let me stay home, but I knew, in his firmness, he
would not.

Knowing I did not have the answer, I turned in my Bible to the
fifteenth chapter of Isaiah. My eyes fell upon the words: "For
the Lord God will help me: therefore shall I not be confounded:

therefore I have set my face like a flint, and I know that I shall not be ashamed. Who is among you that feareth the Lord, that obeyeth the voice of his servant, that walketh in darkness and hath no light? Let him trust in the name of the Lord, and stay upon his God."

I thanked the Lord for this precious promise and felt quite sure that this was His answer and that my duty was to remain faithful to His Word.

"If any of you lack wisdom, let him ask of God, that giveth to all men liberally, and upbraideth not; and it shall be given him."

—JAMES 1:5

Other Character Traits Demonstrated

When Elsie read the passages in the Bible, they spoke directly to her that the Lord was working to make her character like that of Jesus through these trials (which, at first, she thought were from her Papa). Even though it was important that she was reverent to Papa, she also needed to show REVERENCE to her heavenly Father who would be certain to work these things out in her life.

"Therefore, since we are receiving a kingdom that cannot be shaken, let us be thankful, and so worship God acceptably with reverence and awe."

—HEBREWS 12:28, NIV

After Elsie was given the appropriate passages from scripture, she knew in her heart and took it on FAITH that the Lord would help her live with the consequences of the decision she made.

43

The Character of Elsie Dinsmore

"So then faith cometh by hearing and hearing by the word of God."
—ROMANS 10:17

Elsie endeavored to do JUSTICE to the unchanging and eternal commandments the Lord gave her through His Word, by being responsible to follow them as He gave her new strength.

"By myself I can do nothing; I judge only as I hear, and my judgment is just, for I seek not to please myself but him who sent me."
—JOHN 5:30, NIV

Though Elsie struggled through the trial put upon her by Papa to decide between his enduring love that she so desired and faithfulness to her heavenly Father, her ENDURANCE came from the Lord whose very word strengthened her and lifted her out of despair.

"I can do all things through Christ which strengtheneth me."
—PHILIPPIANS 4:13

At first Elsie thought she would have to make her decision right away and did not know how to do this difficult thing, however, the Lord gave her some understanding that He would see her through it in His time. Trusting in His Word, she was able to show PATIENCE while praying about her decision.

"But they that wait upon the LORD shall renew their strength; they shall mount up with wings as eagles; they shall run, and not be weary; and they shall walk, and not faint."
—ISAIAH 40:31

Elsie had a certain DETERMINATION not to be hasty in deciding what to do about this trial Papa had faced her with. It was, after all, too important a decision to be made in haste. Somehow, she was determined to accomplish what her heavenly Father was trying to accomplish through her, without losing Papa forever.

"And every man that striveth for the mastery is temperate in all things. Now they do it to obtain a corruptible crown; but we an incorruptible."

—1 CORINTHIANS 9:25

Character Building Journal

1. In this chapter, you can see how Elsie learned about or applied the positive character trait of DECISIVENESS. In what areas of your life could you put this good character quality into practice? List some ideas in your Journal.

2. In what ways have you exemplified or shown to others this character quality? List them in your Journal.

3. Are there areas of your life that could use a little improvement with regard to DECISIVENESS? List those in your Journal as well and talk with your parents about ways for you to improve in this area.

DEFERENCE

Limiting my freedom in order not to offend the tastes of those God has called me to serve.

Elsie Shows Deference to Miss Day

The day could not have gone worse, even without Arthur's interference. Try as I did to get the lesson right that day, I did not perform the corrections to my lessons to the degree of perfection that Miss Day expected of me.

If only Arthur had not caused me to blot my writing page and had left me alone, I might have done it well enough. I could tell that Arthur was sorry that he spoiled my chance of going riding with the rest. Lora even tried to speak up for me and reveal that it was not my fault, but Miss Day would not hear of it and told Aunt Adelaide I would not be able to go riding with them.

I laid my head upon my desk and struggled hard to keep down the feelings of anger and indignation that were aroused in me by the unjust treatment I had received from Miss Day. When Miss Day came over to confront me about this behavior, I dared not speak in fear that my anger whould show itself in words. So I merely raised my head, and hastily brushing away my tears, I opened my book.

This behavior was an attempt to follow my Lord's example, limiting my freedom so as not to offend Miss Day who was aware that I was a Christian and would not see Jesus in me if I gave a saucy answer.

"It is good neither to eat flesh, nor to drink wine, nor any thing whereby thy brother stumbleth, or is offended, or is made weak."

—ROMANS 14:21

Related Character Trait

In addition to the need to keep from being a poor example of a Christian in front of Miss Day, Elsie was aware of the need to use DISCRETION with her. She needed to be careful to use the right words and show the right attitude, if she did speak with her, or the consequences might be less than desirable. Elsie could see that Miss Day was already pretty upset by Miss Dinsmore.

> *"A prudent man foreseeth the evil, and hideth himself: but the simple pass on, and are punished."*
>
> —PROVERBS 22:3

Elsie Shows More Deference to Miss Day

Some of my greatest challenges to holding my tongue came from encounters with Miss Day. It seemed like she considered it entertainment to be hard on me, whenever possible. However, having been repentant earlier, realizing that speaking some rash words to her was not being like Jesus, as I so desired to be, I found myself needing to hold back.

I had not given Miss Day the smallest excuse for faultfinding the day that she reviewed the work I had redone to perfection for her. The only comments she could find for me were the very cold words, "I see you can do your duties well enough when you choose."

I felt keenly the injustice of that remark and longed to tell her that I had tried quite as earnestly in the morning, but I resolutely crushed down the indignant feeling, and calling to mind the rash words that had cost me so many repentant tears, I replied, "I am sorry I did not succeed better this morning, Miss Day, though I did really try. I am still more sorry for the saucy answer I gave you, and I ask your pardon for it."

"Wherefore, if meat make my brother to offend, I will eat no flesh while the world standeth, lest I make my brother to offend."

—1 CORINTHIANS 8:13

Other Character Traits Demonstrated

Miss Day had been in a very captious mood all day, so Elsie tried her best to use DISCRETION by not giving her the slightest reason to feel provoked. This, she had learned from her Papa as well.

"A man's wisdom gives him patience; it is to his glory to overlook an offense."

—PROVERBS 19:11

Showing MEEKNESS in this incident with Miss Day required that Elsie give up her personal feelings (which she felt she was right about) to the Lord so that He was free to deal with her needs. Elsie should not have expected that the Lord would always give her just what she wanted, just like Papa did not. They both cared for her and how she grew, and giving her what she wanted did not always help her.

"A soft answer turneth away wrath: but grievous words stir up anger."

—PROVERBS 15:1

Elsie was able to do her part, in freeing up Miss Day, by showing Miss Day FORGIVENESS for the actions taken against her earlier that day. Elsie did this by clearing away her memory of the offense and replacing it with a desire for reconciliation through her apology. This helped Miss Day experience God's love as shown through Elsie.

*"Forbearing one another, and forgiving
one another, if any man have a quarrel against any:
even as Christ forgave you, so also do ye."*
—COLOSSIANS 3:13

Elsie Uses Deference around Troubled Adults

It was just one of those days. Miss Day seemed cross; Mrs. Dinsmore was moody and taciturn, complaining of a headache; and Papa was occupied with his morning paper. So the meal passed off in almost unbroken silence.

I was so glad when the meal was over that I hastened to the schoolroom. I thought the best thing to do was to put aside whatever I wanted to do in the free time that I usually had then and get started on my tasks without waiting for the arrival of the regular hour for study.

By giving up my usual freedom, I found I got through my tasks without being disturbed or distracted, by Arthur or anyone, for almost half an hour.

*"Let us not therefore judge one another any more:
but judge this rather, that no man put a stumblingblock
or an occasion to fall in his brother's way."*
—ROMANS 14:13

Related Character Trait

The idea that Elsie knew how to behave around the three adults, while they were in different non-verbal moods, showed a certain amount of RESPONSIBILITY on her part. She was able to realize that the responsible thing to do was to clear out of their way and get started on her daily tasks, without having to be told to do so.

The Character of Elsie Dinsmore

*"For ye had compassion of me in my bonds, and took
joyfully the spoiling of your goods, knowing in yourselves that ye
have in heaven a better and an enduring substance."*

—HEBREWS 10:34

Elsie Shows Deference to Papa

I had sprained my ankle and it hurt terribly, but I did not think
that would be a good excuse not to kneel before the Lord in prayer
at bedtime. However, Papa said I shouldn't try to kneel with my
ankle as it was and that it was alright not to kneel. I told him I
knew that, but I wanted to at least try.

Papa insisted that I either stand by him and say my prayers
while he held me or let him put me in my bed to do so. Realizing
that Papa was only concerned for my condition, I told Papa that I
would pray in my bed.

It was beneficial for me to say my prayers this way, because
Papa sat beside my bed where he could hear my prayers. This gave
me a rare opportunity to discuss the Lord with him that I might
have missed kneeling beside my bed.

*"Although he was a son, he learned obedience
from what he suffered."*

—HEBREWS 5:8, NIV

Related Character Trait

Having to lie in her bed while she prayed gave Elsie the
opportunity to show OBEDIENCE to her Papa. This was one thing
that really pleased him. This opened a door for their conversation
about Jesus.

"Children, obey your parents in all things: for this is well pleasing unto the Lord."

—COLOSSIANS 3:20

Character Building Journal

1.   In this chapter, you can see how Elsie learned about or applied the positive character trait of DEFERENCE. In what areas of your life could you put this good character quality into practice? List some ideas in your Journal.

2.   In what ways have you exemplified or shown to others this character quality? List them in your Journal.

3.   Are there areas of your life that could use a little improvement with regard to DEFERENCE? List those in your Journal as well and talk with your parents about ways for you to improve in this area.

DEPENDABILITY

Fulfilling what I consented to do even if it means unexpected sacrifice.

Elsie Demonstrates Dependability to Lucy

One day, Lucy proposed that we have some candy. I am very fond of candy but explained to her that I would not eat candy without Papa's permission. She immediately suggested that I go ask him, as he was just out on the veranda.

"No," I said to her, "I would rather do without it."

Lucy kept coaxing me to ask him and, seeing that I would not give in, decided to approach Papa on her own. I knew this would not be good.

Lucy asked Papa and was immediately questioned by him.

"Did Elsie send you?" he asked in a cold, grave tone.

"Yes, sir," replied Lucy. She was somewhat frightened, because she had lied.

He then proceeded to tell Lucy to send me to ask for myself. After I went to Papa and was severely reprimanded about sending Lucy instead of coming on my own, I managed to ask if my having some candy would please him. It did not.

I returned sullenly to Lucy who told me that Papa was not very nice and how happy she was that he was not *her* father. Then, Lucy said to me she would buy a bunch of candy tomorrow. Then, we could eat it together, and he would not know. I guess she did not understand fully the principles I live by. I proceeded to explain, "Thank you, Lucy. You can buy candy for yourself if you like, but not for me, for Papa has forbidden me to eat anything of the sort."

"Oh! Of course, we'll not let him know anything about it," Lucy replied.

I just shook my head sadly, saying with a little sigh, "No, Lucy. You are very kind, but I cannot disobey Papa, even if he should never know it. Because that would be disobeying God, and He would know it."

"In whose eyes a vile person is contemned; but he honoureth them that fear the LORD. He that sweareth to his own hurt, and changeth not."

—Psalm 15:4

Related Character Trait

Elsie had a true concern for both what God and her Papa were expecting from her when it came to being obedient to her Papa's wishes about not eating candy. By telling Lucy that her Papa would not know but God would, she demonstrated the admirable character quality of RESPONSIBILITY.

"So then every one of us shall give account of himself to God."

—Romans 14:12

Elsie Shows Her Dependability to Aunt Adelaide

My Aunt Adelaide—who I sometimes call Auntie—and I were planning what I could get Papa for Christmas. I asked her for her opinion, since she was so smart about those kinds of things.

Auntie said that she would think of something presently. After I told her about a couple of things I had thought of, she came up with a grand idea. She thought about me having a miniature of myself made for him.

I was very pleased with this idea, but when she asked how much money I had and I told her, she said it was not quite enough. I was slightly dismayed about that. So with her usual air of generosity, she offered to lend me some money, if necessary.

"Thank you, Auntie," I said gratefully. "You are very kind, but I couldn't take it, because Papa has told me expressly that I must never borrow money, nor run into debt in any way."

"If a man vow a vow unto the LORD, or swear an oath to bind his soul with a bond; he shall not break his word, he shall do according to all that proceedeth out of his mouth."

—NUMBERS 30:2

Related Character Trait

When Elsie politely refused the prospect of borrowing the extra money from her Aunt Adelaide for her Papa's Christmas gift, she showed RESPONSIBILITY by remembering her Papa's directives. He had expressly forbidden her from borrowing money or getting into debt of any kind.

"Who shall give account to him that is ready to judge the quick and the dead."

—1 PETER 4:5

Elsie Shows Her Dependability to Miss Stevens

Miss Stevens was forever trying to pamper me with things that my Papa expressly forbade me to have. She simply did not understand or agree with Papa's strict care for my indulgences and attempted to get around them whenever possible. One day, as I was passing her room upstairs, she called me in.

I regrettably entered, and she asked me to be seated. She went to the dresser, pulled out a large sack of candy, and offered it to me. I was tempted beyond belief, because this was hard to resist for a child my age.

Just that morning, I had prayed hard that the Lord would keep me from temptation and help me to resist such things.

I tried to thank Miss Stevens and began to tell her how Papa did not approve, but she would not hear of it. She insisted, "At least take one or two, child. That much couldn't possibly hurt you, and your Papa need never know."

I could not help myself as I gave her a look of grieved surprise.

"Oh! Could you think I would do that?" I asked her. "But God would know, Miss Stevens; and I should know it myself. How could I ever look my Papa in the face again after deceiving him so?"

"Bread of deceit is sweet to a man; but afterwards his mouth shall be filled with gravel."
—PROVERBS 20:17

Other Character Traits Demonstrated

Again, we see how Elsie showed complete RESPONSIBILITY. This time it was to Miss Stevens, who like several others, tested this quality in Elsie only to find that she was true to it. Elsie knew that it was not a good thing to be tempted to the point of not being trusted to do the right thing.

". . . for we shall all stand before the judgment seat of Christ."
—ROMANS 14:10B

The Character of Elsie Dinsmore

Elsie did not hold back her opinion when it was time to explain to Miss Stevens that TRUTHFULNESS was the best, and in fact, the only way she could go, in good conscience.

"But speaking the truth in love, may grow up into him in all things, which is the head, even Christ."
—EPHESIANS 4:15

Elsie's motives were quite transparent to Miss Stevens concerning the reason she did not want to attempt to eat candy behind her Papa's back. In this manner, Elsie demonstrated her SINCERITY to Miss Stevens and even gave her a look of "grieved surprise" at the notion of committing such a crime.

". . . Abhor that which is evil; cleave to that which is good."
—ROMANS 12:9B

Elsie used DISCRETION with Miss Stevens in using words that did not result in hurt to her and by being very polite while frank about why it would be wrong to accept the candy against the wishes of her Papa. She was successful, in that Miss Stevens was not offended, but rather gave up willingly as she understood that Elsie had a good reason.

"A scorner seeketh wisdom, and findeth it not: but knowledge is easy unto him that understandeth."
—PROVERBS 14:6

Character Building Journal

1. In this chapter, you can see how Elsie learned about or applied the positive character trait of DEPENDABILITY. In what areas of your life could you put this good character quality into practice? List some ideas in your Journal.

2. In what ways have you exemplified or shown to others this character quality? List them in your Journal.

3. Are there areas of your life that could use a little improvement with regard to DEPENDABILITY? List those in your Journal as well and talk with your parents about ways for you to improve in this area.

DETERMINATION

Purposing to accomplish God's goals in God's time regardless of the opposition.

Elsie Shows Determination to Miss Allison

One day, when Miss Allison found me all upset and was trying to console me, she asked me why I was so grieved. I explained to her how I was very much mistreated by Miss Day and had blurted out that I had tried very hard to do my best that day.

Miss Allison thought that my grief was the result of not being able to join the others when they went riding. Though I was very disappointed about that, there was something much more important to me that upset me so.

I explained to Miss Allison the best I could as I showed her the passage in my Bible that I had been reading. "For this is thankworthy, if a man for conscience toward God endure grief, suffering wrongfully. For what glory is it if, when ye be buffeted for your faults, ye shall take it patiently? But if ye do well, and suffer for it, ye take it patiently, this is acceptable with God. For even hereunto ye were called; because Christ also suffered for us, leaving us an example that ye should follow His steps."

"You see? I have not taken it patiently, and I was not following His steps." Then, I cried some more.

"My poor child," she said, passing her arms around my waist, "my poor, little Elsie."

Then Miss Allison read me a passage that told how Christ shed His blood for our sin and explained that He was ready to forgive my sin. Then I explained, "Yes, ma'am. I have asked Him to forgive me, and I know He has. But I am so sorry—oh!—so sorry that I have grieved and displeased Him. For, Miss Allison, I do love Jesus and want to be like Him always!"

> *"I have fought a good fight, I have finished my course,*
> *I have kept the faith."*
>
> —2 TIMOTHY 4:7

Related Character Trait

Along with her determination, Elsie led a sweet life of VIRTUE. She had a moral excellence and purity of spirit that seemed to radiate from her life as she obeyed God's Word and was never content with doing less.

> *"My little children, let us not love in word, neither in tongue;*
> *but in deed and in truth."*
>
> —1 JOHN 3:18

Elsie Shows Determination to Work Harder

I had finished a month's worth of schoolwork that I was less than pleased with and knew that Papa would not be pleased either. Many thoughts ran through my head as I thought to myself about my next month.

I could not remember when I had received such a bad report and could not imagine what had come over me. It seemed as if I could not study and perhaps needed to take a holiday. I thought it might have been caused by laziness. My opinion of laziness was that, if it were so, I must be punished for it.

I really wished I could be rid of this bad habit and feel as industrious as I used to. I resolved to try very hard to do better next month and really felt that I could. After all, it was only one more month until Miss Day would go north for three months, which meant a long holiday for us.

"Surely I can stand one more month," I thought. Even though I felt Papa would not be pleased with this month's report, I said that I would determine to try extra hard next month and that my copy-book would look neat and not have a single blot on it.

"Know ye not that they which run in a race run all, but one receiveth the prize? So run, that ye may obtain."
—1 CORINTHIANS 9:24

Other Character Traits Demonstrated

Elsie showed that she had DILIGENCE by visualizing the task before her in the new month as if it were a special assignment from the Lord. She put a lot of energy into deciding how she was going to accomplish it.

"And whatsoever ye do, do it heartily . . ."
—COLOSSIANS 3:23

Elsie realized that it was through God that she had ENDURANCE. She endured to accomplish tasks that seemed hard for her and did not give up. She set about it and trusted in His strength to get her through.

"But he that shall endure unto the end, the same shall be saved."
—MATTHEW 24:13

Character Building Journal

1. In this chapter, you can see how Elsie learned about or applied the positive character trait of DETERMINATION. In what areas of your life could you put this good character quality into practice? List some ideas in your Journal.

2. In what ways have you exemplified or shown to others this character quality? List them in your Journal.

3. Are there areas of your life that could use a little improvement with regard to DETERMINATION? List those in your Journal as well and talk with your parents about ways for you to improve in this area.

DILIGENCE

Visualizing each task as a special assignment from the Lord and using all my energies to accomplish it.

Elsie Shows Diligence to Miss Day

I always considered my schoolwork important and felt that I must do my very best. Therefore, I set myself to work when Miss Day told us that the quality of our work would determine whether or not we went with her on a ride to the fair that day. I hardly noticed when she instructed Louise and Lora that their French lessons must be perfect.

Then Miss Day addressed me about the expectations of my work that day. I was bent over a slate with the appearance of great industry. "Elsie," she said, "every figure of that example must be correct, your geography lesson recited perfectly, and a page in your copy-book written without a blot."

"Yes, ma'am." I meekly raised my eyes to her face and then instantly dropped them again to my slate.

"Not with eyeservice, as menpleasers; but as the servants of Christ, doing the will of God from the heart."
—EPHESIANS 6:6

Elsie Shows Miss Day Great Diligence

I knew that, though I had really tried to do good work, it was not my fault that my book had been blotted. Now that Arthur was away, I could strive again to do a much better job. There was no one there but me, and I had the time to complete my tasks.

I set to work diligently at my studies and was quite prepared to meet Miss Day when the party returned from the fair. I attended faithfully to all she had required of me. The lesson was recited without the smallest mistake, every figure of the examples worked out correctly, and the page of the copy-book neatly and carefully written.

"With good will do service as to the Lord, and not to men."
—EPHESIANS 6:7

Other Character Traits Demonstrated

Knowing very well that Miss Day would be back before too long from the fair and would expect her to have the lessons rewritten correctly, Elsie set about to have everything right by the time Miss Day returned. In this way, she was able to demonstrate PUNCTUALITY for Miss Day.

". . . for there is a time there for every purpose and for every work."
—ECCLESIASTES 3:17B

Knowing that Miss Day had told her exactly what was expected of her by the time she returned from the fair, Elsie showed RESPONSIBILITY to her tasks. She also had a sense of responsibility to the Lord.

"So then every one of us shall give account of himself to God."
—ROMANS 14:12

Elsie was determined to display THOROUGHNESS, in that she would be demonstrating to Miss Day, her Papa, and the Lord how effective her words as a Christian were by doing what was expected of her.

". . . that ye may stand perfect and complete in all the will of God."
—COLOSSIANS 4:12B

Elsie Showed Diligence in Her Work

Though I was as curious as can be about what it was that was ailing Arthur that day in school when he gruffly turned his back on me for inquiring, I felt it important to give him his space and not press him. It really did grieve me that he reacted so to my kind inquiry, but I was determined to overlook it.

Instead of staring at him or trying to figure it out, I decided to turn my undivided attention to my schoolwork. I was so focused on my tasks that even Miss Day was not able to find fault with me that day.

The reward for paying attention to what I was required to do was forthcoming in the form of a ride with my aunt and Miss Allison and a visit to the fair.

"Looking diligently lest any man fail of the grace of God;
lest any root of bitterness springing up trouble you,
and thereby many be defiled."
—HEBREWS 12:15

Related Character Trait

Elsie demonstrated RESPONSIBILITY, in this instance, by going on with her tasks and completing them, without taking to heart the wrongs that had been committed against her. She knew what was expected from Miss Day, but she did not neglect what her Lord expected of her.

*"Servants, be obedient to them that are your masters
according to the flesh, with fear and trembling, in singleness
of your heart, as unto Christ."*

—EPHESIANS 6:5

Elsie Demonstrated Diligence for Miss Rose

Since Enna had insisted on having the purse that I was making for Miss Rose, I was determined to complete the one that I had been making for Papa to replace it. I gave it to Miss Rose the next morning. She would be leaving then, and I so wanted to give her something made with my own hands. It was important to me, and I knew that she would appreciate a gift like this much more than one that was store-bought.

So, that is just what I did. I was very sad that Miss Rose would be leaving so soon, but I realized that I had no time for crying and that I must keep working on the purse if it was to be done on time. I loved Miss Rose so much that this was not just a task for me but a labor of love.

*"Wherefore seeing we also are compassed about with so
great a cloud of witnesses, let us lay aside every weight, and
the sin which doth so easily beset us,
and let us run with patience the race that is set before us."*

—HEBREWS 12:1

Character Building Journal

1. In this chapter, you can see how Elsie learned about or applied the positive character trait of DILIGENCE. In what areas of your life could you put this good character quality into practice? List some ideas in your Journal.

2. In what ways have you exemplified or shown to others this character quality? List them in your Journal.

3. Are there areas of your life that could use a little improvement with regard to DILIGENCE? List those in your Journal as well and talk with your parents about ways for you to improve in this area.

DISCERNMENT

The God-given ability to understand why things happen.

Elsie Shows Discernment with Papa

I struggled with my feelings about Papa and the punishment I received from him during the remainder of his illness. When he recovered, he did not speak a word to me, and I was deeply saddened by the absence of his affection.

He would not look at me when he joined us for breakfast for the first time in a long while, and I wished that he would come to my room as he used to or that I could have permission to come to visit him in his room.

That morning, my rare plant had blossomed, and I picked off one of the blossoms to take to him. I found an opportunity to come to him sitting in the hall, but he was cold to me and said he was disappointed that I had broken my plant. He sent me away.

I used the time away from him to examine myself and try to determine, through reading my Bible, why this was all happening to me. The Lord never failed to give me the wisdom that I needed through reading His Word.

The Lord revealed to me through scripture that I had been spending less time enjoying Him than in savoring my Papa's love and caresses and that I needed to concentrate more on loving my Savior than on desiring the things of this world. I learned I had been too much engrossed in earthly love and needed a trial to show me that I needed to seek all my happiness in "looking unto Him."

"For the LORD seeth not as man seeth; for man looketh on the outward appearance, but the LORD looketh on the heart."
—1 SAMUEL 16:7B

Character Building Journal

1. In this chapter, you can see how Elsie learned about or applied the positive character trait of DISCERNMENT. In what areas of your life could you put this good character quality into practice? List some ideas in your Journal.

2. In what ways have you exemplified or shown to others this character quality? List them in your Journal.

3. Are there areas of your life that could use a little improvement with regard to DISCERNMENT? List those in your Journal as well and talk with your parents about ways for you to improve in this area.

DISCRETION

The ability to avoid words, actions, and attitudes that could result in undesirable consequences.

Elsie Uses Discretion with Miss Day

I sat and listened as Lora stepped forward to Miss Day and told the truth about how it was not my fault that my book had been blotted and that Arthur was the real culprit in the situation.

Although Lora did her best to convince Miss Day, it did not seem to change my teacher's feelings about me. Miss Day was not about to agree with the idea that she had made a mistake. Instead, after questioning Arthur, she included him in the punishment, which was to miss out on the ride with her to the fair after school.

At this point, while Lora bit her lip to keep from being impertinent with Miss Day, I had a fierce contest with my naturally quick temper. Yet, I felt that it was better not to speak a word or tone or give an expression that would betray the existence of such feelings to Miss Day.

Instead, I sat there at my desk, striving to conquer the feelings of anger and indignation that were swelling in my breast.

"A wise man feareth, and departeth from evil: but the fool rageth, and is confident."

—PROVERBS 14:16

After I had pulled together every ounce of restraint I could to apologize to Miss Day, even when I knew I had been the one who had been wronged, she snapped at me.

"You ought to be sorry," she said and quickly followed that comment with one that said I was "deserving of a much more severe punishment."

The more I thought about the impertinent and impatient way I answered back that morning, the more I felt she was right. But, somehow, the idea that I did not deserve the treatment I received earlier made my eyes swell with tears at her ungracious words.

I felt that the best thing to do was to avoid saying or doing anything that would make things worse between us. I knew she was my appointed teacher and could make my lessons very unpleasant for me. I also knew that the Lord and Papa expected me to do better.

"For his God doth instruct him to discretion, and doth teach him."
—ISAIAH 28:26

Related Character Trait

Elsie had some pretty hard feelings about the way she was being treated by Miss Day, between being accused of what she did not do and having lost her temper earlier and struggling with God over it. Considering these things, she showed considerable SELF-CONTROL after Miss Day's ungracious response to her apology.

"Knowing this, that our old man is crucified with him, that the body of sin might be destroyed, that henceforth we should not serve sin."
—ROMANS 6:6

Elsie Uses Discretion with Mr. Travilla

One day, while Mrs. Travilla sat out on the veranda speaking with Papa, Mr. Travilla began speaking to me about being my new

Papa. I was instantly frightened at the prospect that Papa would just give me away.

It wasn't that I did not like Mr. and Mrs. Travilla, but rather that I could not bear the idea that Papa would even consider giving me away. Mr. Travilla tried to convince me that Papa was thinking about it and, trying to console me, offered that he would "let me have my own way in everything."

"I don't want my own way," I assured Mr. Travilla. "I know it wouldn't always be a good way."

Mr. Travilla prodded me on with, "I thought you liked me." To this, I said, "I like you very much."

"Well, don't you think I would make a good father?" he asked. I was very confused and worried about where this conversation was leading. So, I told him, "I am sure you would be very kind, and that I should love you very much but not so much as I love my own Papa. Because, you know, you are not my Papa, and you never can be, even if he should give me to you."

"As a jewel of gold in a swine's snout, so is a fair woman which is without discretion."

—PROVERBS 11:22

Other Character Traits Demonstrated

Elsie showed SINCERITY in her answers to Mr. Travilla's sweet questions about being a father to her. She really did like him and Mrs. Travilla, though she had little desire to be given to them by her own Papa.

In not wishing to have the life that Mr. Travilla offered her of "having her own way always," Elsie demonstrated her VIRTUE by knowing that it would not be the way that God would have for her life and would not, therefore, be good for her.

"The heart is deceitful above all things, and desperately wicked: who can know it?"

—JEREMIAH 17:9

Character Building Journal

1. In this chapter, you can see how Elsie learned about or applied the positive character trait of DISCRETION. In what areas of your life could you put this good character quality into practice? List some ideas in your Journal.

2. In what ways have you exemplified or shown to others this character quality? List them in your Journal.

3. Are there areas of your life that could use a little improvement with regard to DISCRETION? List those in your Journal as well and talk with your parents about ways for you to improve in this area.

ENDURANCE

The inward strength to withstand stress to accomplish God's best.

Elsie Shows Endurance before Mammy

The struggles I had when my Papa was ill were much greater than just the feelings I had about his poor health. I was dealing with the banishment from Papa because I would not reject one of the Biblical lessons taught to me since infancy and read a worldly book to him on the Sabbath.

Additionally, Aunt Adelaide scolded me severely about my refusal to do so, and to this treatment I felt a faintness come upon me that I could hardly withstand. Practically the entire household blamed me when Papa fell worse, and thus I only had Mammy to console me and help me pray for him and for the strength I needed.

This was a time when I went to the Savior with tears of supplication, and He gave me the strength to grow calm and endure my suffering.

"And let us not be weary in well doing: for in due season
we shall reap, if we faint not."
—GALATIANS 6:9

Other Character Traits Demonstrated

Elsie found her SECURITY not in her immediate surroundings, but rather in those things that are eternal and could not be destroyed or taken away from her.

The Character of Elsie Dinsmore

Elsie made use of her FAITH in the Savior to bring peace in her breast, at a time when there was little or no peace to be found in her immediate surroundings.

The difficulties that were sent Elsie's way during the crises that were going on in the Dinsmore household made it possible for Elsie to demonstrate her utmost LOYALTY to the Lord and her Papa at the same time.

Character Building Journal

1. In this chapter, you can see how Elsie learned about or applied the positive character trait of ENDURANCE. In what areas of your life could you put this good character quality into practice? List some ideas in your Journal.

2. In what ways have you exemplified or shown to others this character quality? List them in your Journal.

3. Are there areas of your life that could use a little improvement with regard to ENDURANCE? List those in your Journal as well and talk with your parents about ways for you to improve in this area.

FAITH

Visualizing what God intends to do in a given situation and acting in harmony with it.

Elsie Reveals Faith to Arthur

It was Arthur's usual style to choose the easiest way, so as to be finished with his lessons. Often I wondered how he even accomplished them to Miss Day's satisfaction. On this day, he could see that I was definitely having a hard time concentrating on the answer to one of my problems. Of course, his answer was to just set down the figures, as I knew the answer, without learning how I arrived at them.

I did not think that was the right thing to do, even if Miss Day would not know. It would be just like telling a white lie, and I told him so. It was my belief that I needed to trust in doing it the honest way, no matter if it caused me to take longer. I knew the Lord would honor that and help me through it.

"Now faith is the substance of things hoped for, the evidence of things not seen."

—HEBREWS 11:1

Other Character Traits Demonstrated

Knowing that telling what she referred to as a "white lie" was not right in the sight of the Lord helped Elsie to demonstrate TRUTHFULNESS to the others. The case was not whether or not Miss Day would know but that God would know. Additionally, Arthur and the others would not be able to trust her from then on, and so her word would lose its value.

*"These are the things that ye shall do;
Speak ye every man the truth to his neighbour;
execute the judgment of truth and peace in your gates."*

—ZECHARIAH 8:16

Because Elsie was able to see the reasoning behind the need to do the lesson truthfully, she was able to demonstrate God's WISDOM. She was able to see the situation from God's point of view.

"And unto man he said, Behold, the fear of the LORD, that is wisdom; and to depart from evil is understanding."

—JOB 28:28

Once again, Elsie showed a good deal of RESPONSIBILITY to Arthur and the others, by not taking advantage of the easy way around the problem. She did what God and those she served expected of her.

". . . and what doth the Lord require of thee, but to do justly, and to love mercy, and to walk humbly with thy God?"

—MICAH 6:8

Elsie Kept the Faith before Lucy

Some of the girls had planned a picnic and a boat ride up the river with Aunt Adelaide, and at first, even I presumed Papa would allow me to go along. Additonally, when I asked Adelaide, she said that she also assumed that I was to be able to go along.

I was looking forward to going, but then Papa came into the room, and Adelaide asked him for permission. Papa said that I was not to go along, but rather I was to stay and do my lessons.

This was so disappointing to me that I cried and went up to my room. Lucy ran up after me, put her arm around me, and said that she would not give it any mind. Then she made a queer statement about how, if she were me, she would go in spite of Papa. I had to set this straight in her mind.

"No, no, Lucy. I must obey my father. God says so, and besides, I couldn't do that if I wanted to."

"My brethren, count it all joy when ye fall into divers temptations; knowing this, that the trying of your faith worketh patience."
—JAMES 1:2-3

Other Character Traits Demonstrated

Elsie was inclined in her MEEKNESS to obey her Papa no matter what her opinion was of his decision to not let her go on the boat ride and picnic. Her justification of such obedience was that "God said so." In her faith, that was the very best reason that could be given.

"Why art thou cast down, O my soul? and why art thou disquieted in me? Hope thou in God: for I shall yet praise him for the help of his countenance."
—PSALM 42:5

Knowing and doing what both God and her Papa were expecting of her was Elsie's RESPONSIBILITY, and she was aware of her need to maintain it. This did not mean that she did not hope to go on the picnic, but that she put her responsibility over her pleasure so that she could find pleasure in what was long lasting.

"The man who plants and the man who waters have one purpose, and each will be rewarded according to his own labor."

—1 CORINTHIANS 3:8, NIV

Showing her commitment to God by letting Lucy know that she must obey her Papa, Elsie was able to demonstrate her strong LOYALTY. This type of commitment was given in the face of a decision that might have been difficult for other children.

"Let no man deceive you with vain words: for because of these things cometh the wrath of God upon the children of disobedience."

—EPHESIANS 5:6

Elsie Shows Her Faith in the Lord

One evening, just at the time I was supposed to go to bed, Papa had become quite taken with Miss Stevens's music, and I did not dare interrupt, though I had hoped to, to receive a goodnight kiss. I had hoped to ask Papa for permission to stay up until one hour later than my usual time, but I did not want to interrupt.

Mr. Travilla, whom I am certain saw my problem, tried to distract me and some other girls in the corner with humorous stories, but my eyes would keep a wandering vigil toward my Papa. I so desired to rescue him away from her.

I eventually gave up the quest as they continued until my bedtime hour, and I went up to my room to retire. Mammy helped me to get ready for bed, and I thought how close Miss Stevens was to Papa this night and how far away I was. I longed to be there close to Papa.

As I knelt down to pray, I became painfully conscious of a feeling of dislike for that lady and felt it creeping into my heart. I asked the Lord earnestly to help me to put this feeling away. I also prayed that I might be spared the trial that I feared. I had determined in my mind that this was because I found out that Miss Stevens was neither good, truthful, nor sincere. I could not tolerate the idea that she might ultimately win my Papa's heart.

Then as I fell asleep, I murmured to myself, "Perhaps dear Papa will come to say goodnight before I am asleep." I was calmed and soothed as I cast my burden on the Lord.

"Casting all your care upon him; for he careth for you."
—1 PETER 5:7

Other Character Traits Demonstrated

Elsie displayed WISDOM in being able to see what she could and could not accomplish in her own strength and allowing the Lord to take the rest.

"The fear of the LORD is the instruction of wisdom; and before honour is humility."
—PROVERBS 15:33

Elsie was able to find great SECURITY in the fact that God's will is done, whether or not the outcome was to her own liking. This was because she found, through faith, that the Lord works all things to good.

"In whom ye also trusted, after that ye heard the word of truth, the gospel of your salvation: in whom also after that ye believed, ye were sealed with that holy Spirit of promise."
—EPHESIANS 1:13

The Character of Elsie Dinsmore

PATIENCE brought Elsie to be able to find sleep, even while she was worried. This kind of patience comes from faith in the Lord's timing and the real hope that her Papa would discover that he forgot to kiss her and come to her, she thought, before she slept for the night.

"Knowing this, that the trying of your faith worketh patience."
—JAMES 1:3

Character Building Journal

1.   In this chapter, you can see how Elsie learned about or applied the positive character trait of FAITH. In what areas of your life could you put this good character quality into practice? List some ideas in your Journal.

2.   In what ways have you exemplified or shown to others this character quality? List them in your Journal.

3.   Are there areas of your life that could use a little improvement with regard to FAITH? List those in your Journal as well and talk with your parents about ways for you to improve in this area.

FORGIVENESS

Clearing the record of those who have wronged me and allowing God to love them through me.

Elsie Shows Forgiveness for Arthur

When the end of the school season arrived, my Papa was presented with my copy-book to examine my progress for the year. I was a bit tense about that one blot, which Arthur had caused me to make, but I knew that Papa would see that I made improvement over last season. I carried my book to him, therefore, with some confidence that it would be well received.

To my extreme surprise, Papa moved angrily through the leaves of my copybook and soon held it up for me to see. I was astonished and baffled to see not one blot, but several blots on every page. I looked my Papa in the eyes and said, "Papa, I did not do it."

Papa was beside himself and asked Miss Day if she could explain how the copy-book got so flawed and added that I denied creating the blots. Miss Day said I was the only one with a key to my desk and could not see how anyone else could have done it. Now, Papa really began to suspect me and truly believed that I was lying to him.

Fearing that Papa would soon be very angry with me, Lora immediately examined the facts of the case, and Arthur entered her mind. She asked him about it, and though he looked very guilty, she could not pry a confession out of him. She then sprang to my side in defense, trying to give all accounts for my good character that she could think of in haste. This seemed to have a decided effect on Papa's understanding, and he chose to believe her. However, he was determined to get to the bottom of the blots and how they got in my book.

After what seemed like a lengthy examination of what I knew about the situation, I was prompted to recall having left the room with my copy-book out one afternoon. Papa then asked me if I knew whether any one else entered the room where I had left my copy-book that day. I thought for a bit and then remembered.

"I do not know, Papa, but I think Arthur must have been in there, because when I came home, I found him reading a book that I had left lying on the mantle-piece," I answered in a low, reluctant tone.

Papa seemed very satisfied that he had discovered the culprit and told me to go along to dinner. But I lingered, and, in an answer to a look of kind inquiry from my Papa, I said to him coaxingly, "Please, Papa, don't be very angry with him. I think he did not know how much I cared about my book."

"And be ye kind one to another, tenderhearted, forgiving one another, even as God for Christ's sake hath forgiven you."
—EPHESIANS 4:32

Character Building Journal

1. In this chapter, you can see how Elsie learned about or applied the positive character trait of FORGIVENESS. In what areas of your life could you put this good character quality into practice? List some ideas in your Journal.

2. In what ways have you exemplified or shown to others this character quality? List them in your Journal.

3. Are there areas of your life that could use a little improvement with regard to FORGIVENESS? List those in your Journal as well and talk with your parents about ways for you to improve in this area.

GENEROSITY

Realizing that all I have belongs to God and using it for His purposes.

Elsie Shows Generosity to Papa

After Papa had been away for so very long, I decided to prepare something very special for him on his return. News of his return had gotten me very excited, and I found it hard to contain myself. Mrs. Dinsmore had to tell me to stop skipping around the house and to act more like a lady.

As Papa arrived home, I greeted him with many hugs and kisses, which he also returned. It was chilly out, so he took me by the hand and led me inside, while the servants attended to his bags.

Aunt Adelaide helped me earlier to make sure that there was a bright, warm fire in Papa's dressing room. In addition to this, his large easy chair was drawn up near the fireplace, and a handsome dressing-gown and slippers were just where I had placed them. All this was the work of my little hands and had been prepared in love to be just right for Papa. I so cared that my Papa would be comfortable after he returned. What I gave that day was nothing in comparison to what I received from having him there with me again and seeing that he enjoyed what I had prepared for him.

"But this I say, He which soweth sparingly shall reap also sparingly; and he which soweth bountifully shall reap also bountifully."
—2 CORINTHIANS 9:6

Other Character Traits Demonstrated

Elsie had true LOVE for her Papa and demonstrated that love by wanting to do things to please him. She was concerned for his comfort and looked after his basic needs. Although his kind reaction did fulfill certain basic needs in Elsie for his affection, it was not usually her motive for serving him this way.

"Love . . . never seeks its own advantage . . ."
—1 CORINTHIANS 13:4-5, NJB

Elsie usually showed a certain personal care and concern for the needs of other people. This unique GENTLENESS was a mark of her special Christ-like character that revealed itself in her relationship with adversaries, as well as those she loved.

". . . in all things I have kept myself from being burdensome unto you, and so will I keep myself."
—2 CORINTHIANS 11:9B

Elsie Shows Generosity for the Servants

The servants of the Dinsmore household did not seem like servants to me. They were the most down-to-earth people there. They did not seem to have high thoughts about who they were and did not have demands as to a special way in which they were to be treated. And then there was Mammy, who was genuinely like a mamma to me.

I did not find it difficult to like them and was mindful that I would want to buy each and every one of them a special gift for Christmas. I enjoyed making out a list of the articles that would be suitable for each. However, as I was leaving to go shopping, I counted how much money I had left and determined that after I had spent so much on the hand-painted miniature portrait for Papa, I did not have much left.

This thought made me feel sad as I went down to get in the carriage. I so wanted to buy the servants some nice gifts. There, waiting at the carriage, was Papa, who said he could not come with me but unexpectedly placed a twenty-dollar gold piece in my hand.

"Give, and it shall be given unto you; good measure, pressed down, and shaken together, and running over, shall men give into your bosom. For with the same measure that ye mete withal it shall be measured to you again."

—LUKE 6:38

Another Related Character Trait

Often at Christmas, we all have a tendency to give to others. However, Elsie's generosity showed how much she had LOVE for the household servants. She felt actual gloom at the idea that she may not be able to fulfill their needs.

"What doth it profit, my brethren, though a man say he hath faith, and have not works? Can faith save him?"

—JAMES 2:14

Elsie Again Shows Generosity to the Servants

It was a great Christmas when I was given the opportunity to present gifts to the household servants. I had already given Papa the slippers I had sewn with my very own hands.

After breakfast, the household servants were all called in to family worship, as usual. When that had been attended to, I went over to a large basket and uncovered it.

I am sure my face must have been beaming with the delight that was in my heart as I passed out the Christmas gifts. There was a nice, new calico dress or a bright-colored handkerchief for each person accompanied by a paper of confectionery.

The Character of Elsie Dinsmore

"The liberal soul shall be made fat: and he that watereth shall be watered also himself."

—PROVERBS 11:25

Character Building Journal

1. In this chapter, you can see how Elsie learned about or applied the positive character trait of GENEROSITY. In what areas of your life could you put this good character quality into practice? List some ideas in your Journal.

2. In what ways have you exemplified or shown to others this character quality? List them in your Journal.

3. Are there areas of your life that could use a little improvement with regard to GENEROSITY? List those in your Journal as well and talk with your parents about ways for you to improve in this area.

GRATEFULNESS

Making known to God and others in what ways they have benefited my life.

Elsie Shows Gratefulness to Pomp

Many times, the household servants just did as they were asked, and we sort of imagined that that was just how things were. I don't remember any of the Dinsmores giving them even a simple thanks for waiting on them or attending to the house and their every need.

One of the servants, Pomp, brought a very nice dinner up to my room, where Papa had sent me as punishment. Though it was not customary, I said to Pomp, "Papa is very good, and I am much obliged to you, too, Pomp."

I think this pleased Pomp very much, because he said I was welcome and left the room with a very large grin on his face.

"For who maketh thee to differ from another? And what hast thou that thou didst not receive? Now if thou didst receive it, why dost thou glory, as if thou hadst not received it?"
—1 CORINTHIANS 4:7

Elsie Shows Gratefulness to Papa

One day before Christmas, Miss Caroline, who I call Carry, and I were discussing the idea of going shopping. I felt sure that Papa would take us and proceeded to ask him. His reply, however, indicated that he had a business engagement and could not take us.

After a short moment, I asked him if we could use one of the carriages. Perhaps Pomp or Ajax could drive us. Papa did not like the idea at all and felt that it would not be good to send us alone with a servant to town.

I forgot myself for just a moment in my determination to go and pleaded again that I believed that we would be just fine. Papa was not pleased with this pleading and reminded me that once he decided to say no, I should not ask again.

I blushed and hung my head, but at that moment Aunt Adelaide offered to take Carry and me shopping with her. Papa saw this as a way to solve the dilemma and said I may go, if Carry had her mother's permission.

I was very pleased and grateful and told Papa, "Thank you, dear Papa. Thank you so very much."

> *". . . give thanks in all circumstances, for this is God's will for you in Christ Jesus."*
> —I THESSALONIANS 5:18, NIV

Elsie Shows More Gratefulness to Papa

It had been a great and gleeful Christmas day. All the children were very excited to see the beautiful tree so brightly decorated. They clapped and danced around at seeing the toys and bonbons and handsomely wrapped gifts. Soon Mrs. Dinsmore and Adelaide began distributing the gifts all around, calling the names out one at a time.

Everyone had received gifts purchased especially for them. I received a wonderful bracelet from my Aunt Adelaide, a needle case from Aunt Lora, and several little gifts from my young guests. But, I was beginning to wonder what had become of Papa's promised present, when my name rang out once more.

Just as I turned around, Aunt Adelaide slipped the most beautiful diamond ring on my finger. She said it was from my Papa and that I should go and thank him.

I found him in the corner enjoying the sight of all the commotion and said to him, "See, Papa. I think it is very beautiful. Thank you, dear Papa. Thank you very much." I told him it was the prettiest ring I had ever seen. I was truly grateful to Papa for expressing his love and approval of me through such a valuable gift.

"For everything God created is good, and nothing is to be rejected if it is received with thanksgiving."
—1 TIMOTHY 4:4, NIV

Character Building Journal

1. In this chapter, you can see how Elsie learned about or applied the positive character trait of GRATEFULNESS. In what areas of your life could you put this good character quality into practice? List some ideas in your Journal.

2. In what ways have you exemplified or shown to others this character quality? List them in your Journal.

3. Are there areas of your life that could use a little improvement with regard to GRATEFULNESS? List those in your Journal as well and talk with your parents about ways for you to improve in this area.

HUMILITY

Recognizing that God and others are actually responsible for the achievements in my life.

Elsie Shows Humility before Lora

Aunt Lora and I were walking back to the house from where, moments before, our very lives seemed to flash before us. The horses pulling our carriage had gotten frightened and sent us sailing full speed—certainly to a disastrous end—until the Lord sent us a brave man to rescue our lives at the risk of his own.

Lora could not seem to stop talking and went on about how terribly frightened she and the others were and how I seemed to be the only one that wasn't afraid. As I turned over the leaves of my Bible, I explained to her.

"I was thinking of this sweet verse: 'Yea, though I walk through the valley of the shadow of death, I will fear no evil; for thou art with me.' Oh, Lora! It made me so happy to think that Jesus was there with me and that if I were killed, I should only fall asleep to wake up again in His arms. Then how could I be afraid?"

Lora asked me if I did not feel afraid for her and the others, because, as she explained, they were not Christians nor pretended to be. I was very embarrassed and confessed that it happened so fast that I had been afraid only for my Papa who would miss me dearly. Then I told her, "I was very selfish, I know. But, it was only for a moment."

"But he giveth more grace. Wherefore he saith, God resisteth the proud, but giveth grace unto the humble."

—JAMES 4:6

Other Character Traits Demonstrated

Elsie spoke with TRUTHFULNESS to her Aunt Lora when she admitted she was being selfish in just thinking about herself and her Papa, as far as where her soul would be if they had been killed in the carriage mishap. This sort of truthfulness earned her a reputation as someone very trustworthy.

"The lip of truth shall be established for ever: but a lying tongue is but for a moment."

—PROVERBS 12:19

Using her SENSITIVITY, Elsie was able to tell that Lora was hurt by the fact that Elsie thought of the possibility of her Papa being lost without his daughter around to tell him about Jesus but neglected to think what would have been the case with the other girls. They, admittedly, did not know Jesus either. This prepared Elsie to quickly attend to Lora's aching heart and spiritual needs through her sensitive heart.

"And whether one member suffer, all the members suffer with it; or one member be honored, all the members rejoice with it."

—1 CORINTHIANS 12:26

Elsie Shows Humility to a Gentleman

One evening, Papa had some gentlemen friends to the house and was sitting with them discussing religion. I was sitting, at the time, on my Papa's knee as they turned to a discussion about whether or not a change of heart was necessary for salvation.

The general opinion seemed to be that it was not, and I listened with pain as my father expressed his decided conviction that all who led an honest, upright, moral life and attended to the outward observances of religion were quite safe.

One of the guests expressed that he agreed with Papa and noticed the mournful look on my face. He remarked that I looked as though I had an opinion on the subject. This caught me by surprise, as I blushed and looked to Papa. Papa told me to go ahead and say what was on my mind.

I told the gentleman of what the Savior said to Nicodemus about having to be born again to enter the kingdom of God. The gentleman asked what was meant by "being born again." I explained it meant to have a clean heart, as David had.

The gentleman inquired as to where I learned this. I told him it was from the Bible. He then asked me how this change occurs. I told him by the Holy Spirit. He went on to ask, "How am I to secure His aid?" I told him it was by asking.

Then he turned the question to me and inquired, "Have you obtained this new heart, Miss Elsie?" I told him that I hoped that I had, and he reapplied the question. "Why do you think so?" He went on to support the question by reminding me that the Bible says I must be able to give a reason for the hope that is in me.

Then, raising my eyes to his face, with humility and some boldness, I said, "And this, sir, is my answer. Jesus says: 'Him that cometh unto me, I will in no wise cast him out,' and I believe Him. I did go to Him, and He did not cast me out but forgave my sins and taught me to love Him and desire to serve Him all my life."

"The fear of the LORD is the instruction of wisdom; and before honour is humility."

—PROVERBS 15:33

Other Character Traits Demonstrated

Elsie used PERSUASIVENESS in humbly using her knowledge of scripture and the leading of the Holy Spirit to guide God's vital truths around the mental stumbling blocks of the gentleman questioning her about salvation and perhaps those of the gentlemen hearing her.

"Holding fast the faithful word as he hath been taught, that he may be able by sound doctrine both to exhort and to convince the gainsayers."

—TITUS 1:9

When it came time to speak, just a young girl among men and her Papa, Elsie somehow found the BOLDNESS to speak what was true, right, and just in the sight of God. This took unusual courage that could only have come from the Lord.

". . . and they were all filled with the Holy Ghost, and they spake the word of God with boldness."

—ACTS 4:31

These men could certainly see VIRTUE in Elsie as she spoke to them the words of the Bible. The gentleman, at one point, even remarked about her countenance by stating that she seemed to have read about salvation and a clean heart "to some purpose."

"But grow in grace, and in the knowledge of our Lord and Saviour Jesus Christ. To him be glory both now and for ever. Amen."

—2 PETER 3:18

Character Building Journal

1.   In this chapter, you can see how Elsie learned about or applied the positive character trait of HUMILITY. In what areas of your life could you put this good character quality into practice? List some ideas in your Journal.

2.   In what ways have you exemplified or shown to others this character quality? List them in your Journal.

3.   Are there areas of your life that could use a little improvement with regard to HUMILITY? List those in your Journal as well and talk with your parents about ways for you to improve in this area.

INITIATIVE

*Recognizing and doing what needs to be done
before I am asked to do it.*

Elsie Shows Initiative to Mammy

Mammy was always doing things for me, helping me, and making sure I did everything that I was supposed to do during the day. She was always there at my side and lovingly guided me through my days.

I really did love Mammy and appreciated her being there for me as I grew. I knew the feeling she had toward me was the same, and so we were just like mother and daughter.

One evening, while Mammy was brushing back her own hair and putting it under her nightcap, having already helped me get dressed for bed, I went ahead, knelt down, and said my prayers. Then, I came back to the night table next to the bed where she slept and told her I was going to read a chapter from the Bible to her while she finished preparing herself for bed.

"Be not overcome of evil, but overcome evil with good."
—ROMANS 12:21

Related Character Trait

Elsie chose with all SINCERITY to do what was right in the eyes of her Lord. She did not have any hope of personal gain by reading the Bible to Mammy. She wanted only to serve Mammy, as she had been served, in a way that a little girl of eight or nine could do.

"But as touching brotherly love ye need not that I write unto you: for ye yourselves are taught of God to love one another."

—1 THESSALONIANS 4:9

Character Building Journal

1. In this chapter, you can see how Elsie learned about or applied the positive character trait of INITIATIVE. In what areas of your life could you put this good character quality into practice? List some ideas in your Journal.

2. In what ways have you exemplified or shown to others this character quality? List them in your Journal.

3. Are there areas of your life that could use a little improvement with regard to INITIATIVE? List those in your Journal as well and talk with your parents about ways for you to improve in this area.

JUSTICE

Personal responsibility to God's unchanging laws.

Elsie Uses Justice to Correct Her Own Behavior

There are some things that I struggled with as a Christian that, in looking back, I am sure were necessary hardships. I had a streak of stubbornness and impatience that I continuously had to subdue in order to fulfill my desire to be like Jesus.

One person who seemed to win the prize for being able to pull these unwanted flaws to the surface was Miss Day. I had no desire to be at odds with Miss Day. However, it always seemed that she had that very thing in mind for me. I forever seemed the odd child to her and could not seem to please her.

I already felt very mistreated and wronged by Arthur one morning. Miss Day was irritated with Mrs. Dinsmore and was looking for someone upon whom to vent this frustration. She asked me, in a demanding tone, if she had not told me to learn my lesson over. I was afraid to speak, dreading the probable consequences and that my angry feelings might come out. But, she decided to take me by the arm and shake it out of me, while inquiring, "Why have you been idling all the morning?"

This was a little more than I could bear. So, before I knew it, I blurted out at her, "I have not. I have tried hard to do my duty, and you are punishing me when I don't deserve it at all." As one could expect, this was not the way to Miss Day's heart. As a matter of fact, she boxed one of my ears.

Although I was very upset, I intensely held back, but the tears in my eyes made it hard to see my studies. I waited until all had gone, so that I could release my tears in solitude.

97

This is when I realized that the Bible spoke plainly about this situation. I turned its pages to a verse and read: "For this is thankworthy, if a man for conscience toward God endure grief, suffering wrongfully. For what glory is it if, when ye be buffeted for your faults, ye shall take it patiently? But if when ye do well, and suffer for it, ye take it patiently, this is acceptable with God. For even hereunto were ye called; because Christ also suffered for us, leaving us an example that ye should follow His steps."

I realized at once that I did not suffer patiently when treated unjustly, and therefore, I was not really following in His steps as it said and as I so desired to do.

"He hath shewed thee, O man, what is good; and what doth the LORD require of thee, but to do justly, and to love mercy, and to walk humbly with thy God?"

—MICAH 6:8

Related Character Trait

Elsie demonstrated great SELF-CONTROL after her outburst by listening to the Holy Spirit's prompting not to make a still more angry reply to Miss Day after she struck her on the ear. Instead, she showed practiced restraint and turned immediately to her books and her studies.

"For as many as are led by the Spirit of God, they are the sons of God."

—ROMANS 8:14

Elsie Shows Justice before Adelaide

I believe my dear Aunt Adelaide suffered my punishments from Papa to some degree more than I did myself. She would always, it seemed, come behind the scene to give voice to what she thought were the rebellious words I must be thinking, though that was not usually the case.

I loved Aunt Adelaide all the same. I just tried not to give in to her temptations and to do what Papa commanded me not to do. She would usually tempt me by saying that Papa would never find out. However, I would thank her and tell her the reason for my conviction.

On a particular day, she came to my room, where I was confined. I knew something was going on in her mind when she locked the door behind her. She had an air of secrecy about her that caught my curiosity. But soon, she revealed a letter. It was from Miss Rose. She knew that I would want to read it and told me that I could read it. She said she would never tell Papa. What was more, thinking that I would be afraid Papa would find out, she suggested we destroy the letter after I read it. She offered also to write Miss Rose herself and suggest that she not write again to save me from suspicion.

It was an awful temptation to me, but I told her it would be wrong of me to touch the letter while Papa was against it. Adelaide pleaded with me, insisting that she would never tell and Papa would not find out, but I explained to her, "I am not at all afraid to trust you, Aunt Adelaide, nor do I think there is any danger of Papa's finding it out. But, I should know it myself, and God would know it, too, and you know He has commanded me to obey my father in everything that is not wrong. I must obey him, no matter how hard it is."

*"But let judgment run down as waters, and righteousness
as a mighty stream."*
—AMOS 5:24

Other Character Traits Demonstrated

By knowing and doing what God and her Papa were expecting of her in the situation with the letter, Elsie demonstrated RESPONSIBILITY to Adelaide. She held herself responsible even when her papa was not there to see her do so.

"Which show the work of the law written in their hearts, their conscience also bearing witness, and their thoughts the mean while accusing or else excusing one another."

—ROMANS 2:15

Elsie admitted being sorely tempted by the letter that she dearly longed to read from Miss Rose, however, during this difficult time, she showed her LOYALTY to her Lord and to her Papa whom the Lord wished her to serve.

"But ye, brethren, be not weary in well doing."

—2 THESSALONIANS 3:13

Character Building Journal

1. In this chapter, you can see how Elsie learned about or applied the positive character trait of JUSTICE. In what areas of your life could you put this good character quality into practice? List some ideas in your Journal.

2. In what ways have you exemplified or shown to others this character quality? List them in your Journal.

3. Are there areas of your life that could use a little improvement with regard to JUSTICE? List those in your Journal as well and talk with your parents about ways for you to improve in this area.

LOVE

Giving to others' basic needs without having as my motive personal reward.

Elsie Shows Love to Arthur

I had an unspoken desire to return good for the bad that Arthur had done to me over a period of time. One day, when he came to me and said he saw a beautiful sailboat that he wanted badly but could not afford, his mournful comment provided the perfect opportunity for me to give him the money. He asked me for a loan that he could pay back, but I thought it would be a good turn to purchase it as a gift for him. I thought that, as a surprise, it might be even more appreciated.

The plan sailed along as smoothly as the ship, and he was most surprised and grateful to me. I really was delighted to see him so happy and, though I did not have it in mind to receive anything in return for the gift, I did gain the pleasure of giving.

However, Arthur did not exactly understand that it was a gift and told me that he would pay me back when he got his allowance.

"Oh, no!" I explained to him. "That would spoil it all, Arthur. You are entirely welcome, and you know my allowance is so large that half the time I have more money than I know how to spend."

"And though I bestow all my goods to feed the poor, and though I give my body to be burned, and have not charity, it profiteth me nothing."

—1 CORINTHIANS 13:3

Related Character Trait

Elsie had a special part of her makeup that displayed the character of VIRTUE by radiating God's innocence and the love that stems from obeying Him and always attempting to follow in His steps. As David, Elsie also had a heart after God.

"But we all, with open face beholding as in a glass the glory of the Lord, are changed into the same image from glory to glory, even as by the Spirit of the Lord."
—2 CORINTHIANS 3:18

Character Building Journal

1. In this chapter, you can see how Elsie learned about or applied the positive character trait of LOVE. In what areas of your life could you put this good character quality into practice? List some ideas in your Journal.

2. In what ways have you exemplified or shown to others this character quality? List them in your Journal.

3. Are there areas of your life that could use a little improvement with regard to LOVE? List those in your Journal as well and talk with your parents about ways for you to improve in this area.

LOYALTY

Using difficult times to demonstrate my commitment to God and to those whom He has called me to serve.

Elsie Demonstrates Loyalty to Louise

Arthur could be an absolute pest sometimes, and I figured he must have been sent into my life to build character. During school, especially when Miss Day stepped out of the class, he usually increased his pestering.

It was just such a day, and I was especially concerned about getting my lessons done. I did so want to go for a ride with the others to the fair that afternoon.

I am not sure whether Arthur wanted me to miss my lesson or he just liked to tease me, but he simply would not let me alone with my lesson. I explained to him that I would never be able to get my lesson right with him bothering me so. Yet, he just kept on tickling me, pulling my hair, and twitching the book out of my hand. He kept on talking to me, making remarks or asking me questions, until I complained that he would have to let me alone.

Louise, trying to be helpful, suggested that I go out on the veranda to finish my lessons and said she would call me back when Miss Day was coming.

"Oh, no, Louise!" I told her. "I cannot do that, because it would be disobedience."

"Greater love hath no man than this, that a man lay down his life for his friends."

—JOHN 15:13

Related Character Trait

Elsie believed that OBEDIENCE was greater in importance to God than sacrifice. She would never have even considered the question of disobeying Miss Day or anyone else in authority, unless she was asked to do something contrary to Scripture.

"By whom we have received grace and apostleship, for obedience to the faith among all nations, for his name."

—ROMANS 1:5

Elsie Showed Loyalty within Her Desires

When the time came for Miss Rose Allison to leave the Dinsmore home, I was very sorrowful and knew that I would miss her. There was little I could do except bear the pain I felt because I missed her so much.

Right away, I found myself on my knees with my Bible opened before me. I poured out the story of my sins and sorrows to the ears of my dear Savior whom I love so well. I confessed that I had not taken this trial patiently and earnestly pleaded that I might be made more like the meek and lowly Jesus.

Quiet sobs burst from my burdened heart, and the tears of my penitence fell upon the pages of the Holy Book.

As I rose from my knees, the load of the sin and sorrow was all gone. My heart was made light and happy with the sense of peace and pardon. Again, I experienced the blessedness of "the man whose transgression is forgiven, whose sin is covered."

"And walk in love, as Christ also hath loved us, and hath given himself for us an offering and a sacrifice to God for a sweet smelling savour."

—EPHESIANS 5:2

Related Character Trait

Elsie became aware of how God had used Miss Allison and others in her life to begin to make her more like Christ. In her REVERENCE, she saw that she needed this change and that it was good and necessary in her life.

"So shall the knowledge of wisdom be unto thy soul: when thou hast found it, then there shall be a reward, and thy expectation shall not be cut off."

—PROVERBS 24:14

Elsie Shows Enna Loyalty to the Lord

I once learned a fairy tale that I grew to wish I had never learned. Enna was feeling ill and, as I had chosen to stay home from riding with my Papa, she asked me to tell the story to her. It happened that it was the Sabbath, and I knew that I must remain loyal to the Lord and not read such a tale on His day. However, Enna, really wanting to hear the fairy tale, demanded that I tell it to her. I told her that I could not tell her the story on the Sabbath. So, Enna sprang to her feet to run and complain to Mrs. Dinsmore. Trying to be true to my convictions, I tried to reason with her.

"Stay, Enna," I said, catching her hand to detain her. "I will tell you any story I know that is suitable for the Sabbath, but I cannot tell the fairy tale today, because you know it would be wrong. I will tell it to you tomorrow, though, if you will wait."

"I am crucified with Christ: nevertheless I live; yet not I, but Christ liveth in me: and the life which I now live in the flesh I live by the faith of the Son of God, who loved me, and gave himself for me."

—GALATIANS 2:20

105

Other Character Traits Demonstrated

Elsie showed RESPONSIBILITY to her God by only doing things that He expected her to do on the Sabbath. This responsible attitude came at a great cost to her personal freedom, yet it was more important to her.

> *". . . I am he who searches hearts and minds, and I will repay each of you according to your deeds."*
> —REVELATION 2:23B, NIV

In her BOLDNESS, Elsie was confident that what she had to say to Enna, about reading fairy tales on the Sabbath, was true and right and just in the eyes of God.

> *"Be not afraid, but speak, and hold not thy peace."*
> —ACTS 18:9

Elsie knew that Enna had many mental roadblocks that often got in the way of her understanding what was right and true. She knew it would take some PERSUASIVENESS to help her understand why it was not right for her to tell the fairy tale on the Sabbath.

> *"Brethren, if any of you do err from the truth, and one convert him."*
> —JAMES 5:19

Character Building Journal

1. In this chapter, you can see how Elsie learned about or applied the positive character trait of LOYALTY. In what areas of

your life could you put this good character quality into practice? List some ideas in your Journal.

2. In what ways have you exemplified or shown to others this character quality? List them in your Journal.

3. Are there areas of your life that could use a little improvement with regard to LOYALTY? List those in your Journal as well and talk with your parents about ways for you to improve in this area.

MEEKNESS

Yielding my personal rights and expectations to God.

Elsie Shows Meekness to Her Offenders

After I bought Arthur the ship he wanted and did not expect him to pay me back, he was quite good to me for many weeks. However, this did not keep the others such as Miss Day, Walter, or Enna from making life as difficult as possible for me.

There was scarcely a day in which I was not called upon to yield my own wishes or pleasures to please Walter, Enna, and occasionally the elder members of the family. Even still, Miss Rose Allison's love and uniform kindness shed sunlight on my path.

I learned to yield readily to others, and when I fretted or was saddened by unjust or unkind treatment, a few moments alone with my Bible and my Savior made everything right again. I would come singing from those sweet communings, causing the whole family to wonder about me. It absolutely astonished old Mr. Dinsmore to see me give up my own wishes to Enna without a frown or a pout.

> *"My soul, wait thou only upon God; for my expectation is from him."*
>
> —PSALM 62:5

Elsie Shows Meekness to Miss Day

I had striven long and hard to show a good report to Papa, so that he would be pleased with me. However, this one morning, Miss Day was in a very bad humor. She was peevish, fretful, irritable, and I might say unreasonable to the last degree.

As usual, I became the principle sufferer of her ill humor. She found fault with every single thing that I did—scolding me, shaking me, refusing to explain the manner of working out a very difficult example or permit me to apply to anyone else for assistance, and then punishing me because it was done incorrectly. When I could no longer keep back tears, she called me a baby for crying and a dunce for not understanding my arithmetic better.

Through all this, I did not answer a word, yielding it in my heart to the Lord.

"It is better to trust in the LORD than to put confidence in man."

—PSALM 118:8

Related Character Trait

Elsie demonstrated great PATIENCE while waiting for the Lord to act in His own time to bring her out of this painful environment. She had faith that all would result in good in the end and that she would be more like Jesus as a result.

"Therefore I take pleasure in infirmities, in reproaches, in necessities, in persecutions, in distresses for Christ's sake: for when I am weak, then am I strong."

—2 CORINTHIANS 12:10

Elsie Shows Meekness to Mr. Travilla

One day Mr. Travilla, quite out of concern for me and my Papa, tried to persuade me that to sin in a small way against God to please my Papa and appease the situation at hand between us would certainly be a compromise acceptable to God.

"Mr. Travilla," I said to him in a tone of deep solemnity, "it is written, 'Curse be everyone that continueth not in all things which are written on the book of the law to do them.' That is in the Bible, and the catechism says: 'Every sin deserveth the wrath and curse of God!' Oh, Mr. Travilla, if you only knew how very hard it is for me to keep from giving up and doing what my conscience says is wrong, you wouldn't try to persuade me to do it!"

"As you know, we consider blessed those who have persevered. You have heard of Job's perseverance and have seen what the Lord finally brought about. The Lord is full of compassion and mercy."
—JAMES 5:11, NJB

Character Building Journal

1.   In this chapter, you can see how Elsie learned about or applied the positive character trait of MEEKNESS. In what areas of your life could you put this good character quality into practice? List some ideas in your Journal.

2.   In what ways have you exemplified or shown to others this character quality? List them in your Journal.

3.   Are there areas of your life that could use a little improvement with regard to MEEKNESS? List those in your Journal as well and talk with your parents about ways for you to improve in this area.

OBEDIENCE

*Freedom to be creative under the protection of
divinely appointed authority.*

Elsie Demonstrates Obedience for Miss Rose

It had been quite a long and trying day for me. First, Arthur set me on the wrong track with Miss Day by causing me to blot my copy-book, and then I was made to stay behind as they all rode to the fair, while I did my lessons over to Miss Day's perfection.

When they returned, I had finished the work as I was required but still had to make my apologies to Miss Day. She responded in such an unkind and ungracious manner that it took me by surprise.

I had decided it best not to respond in kind but to be obedient to the one who was placed in charge of my teaching. Without a word, I placed my books and slate carefully on my desk and left the room.

I remembered my appointment to meet with Miss Rose Allison in her room to read the Bible with her. She answered the door, and I went in and sat down on the low ottoman—the one pointed out by Miss Rose. Then I made sure I said to her, "I may stay with you for half an hour, Miss Allison, if you like, and then Mammy is coming to put me to bed."

*"Casting down imaginations, and every high thing that exalteth
itself against the knowledge of God, and bringing into captivity
every thought to the obedience of Christ."*
—2 CORINTHIANS 10:5

Related Character Trait

Elsie was able to demonstrate her PUNCTUALITY to Miss Allison—first by being at her room on time and then for setting a time limit, so as not to waste Mammy's time. This was a way of showing that she had high regard for other peoples' time.

"Make the best of the present time, for it is a wicked age."
—EPHESIANS 5:16, NJB

Elsie Shows Arthur Her Obedience

One morning over breakfast, Papa overheard Arthur mocking me by saying, "Isn't it delightful having your Papa at home, Elsie? It's very pleasant to live on bread and water. Isn't it, eh?"

I was very quick to set him on the right understanding. "I don't live on bread and water. Papa always allows me to have as much good, rich milk, cream, and fruit as I want, or I can have eggs, cheese, honey, or anything else—except meat, hot cakes, butter, and coffee. Who wouldn't rather do without such things all their lives than not have a Papa to love them?"

"But whoever listens to me will live in safety and be at ease, without fear of harm."
—PROVERBS 1:33, NJB

Elsie Shows Lucy Her Obedience

Lucy and Carry were at the house as my guests one day when Lucy, standing at the window, saw Miss Adelaide and Miss Stevens bringing the horses out to go riding. She remarked how beautiful Miss Adelaide was in her riding dress and cap. She also commented about Miss Stevens and how hateful she was and revealed that she could not bear her.

As she ran out yelling, "Come girls, let us run out and see them off," both Carry and I ran after her. However, I stopped short at the front stoop. They called for me to come, and I said that I could not come without a wrap around me.

I explained quickly that Papa said it was too cold for me to be out in the wind that day with my neck and arms bare. Lucy said that it was not cold at all, and I politely told her, "No, Lucy, I must obey my father."

> *"Although he was a son, he learned obedience*
> *from what he suffered."*
> —HEBREWS 5:8, NIV

Other Character Traits Demonstrated

Though Elsie was, to her knowledge, alone with her two young friends, she did not succumb to temptation but showed RESPONSIBILITY toward her Papa. She remembered his words to her about the wind and realized that he was trying to protect her and that she needed to remain obedient.

> *"For every man shall bear his own burden."*
> —GALATIANS 6:5

Elsie had a commitment to God and her Papa to show them LOYALTY. She made up her mind to keep this commitment even to the point of being thought nonsensical to her friends.

> *"And walk in love, as Christ also hath loved us, and*
> *hath given Himself for us an offering*

and a sacrifice for God for a sweet smelling savour."

—EPHESIANS 5:2

Character Building Journal

1. In this chapter, you can see how Elsie learned about or applied the positive character trait of OBEDIENCE. In what areas of your life could you put this good character quality into practice? List some ideas in your Journal.

2. In what ways have you exemplified or shown to others this character quality? List them in your Journal.

3. Are there areas of your life that could use a little improvement with regard to OBEDIENCE? List those in your Journal as well and talk with your parents about ways for you to improve in this area.

ORDERLINESS

*Preparing my surroundings and myself so that
I will achieve the greatest efficiency.*

Elsie Demonstrates Orderliness

In thinking about how my report would come out, I decided, on the day that school was closing, to organize my books and things. I stayed after everyone had left to carefully arrange the books, writing, drawing materials, and such in my desk. Out of habit, I felt like everything had to be neat and orderly.

"Let all things be done decently and in order."
—1 CORINTHIANS 14:40

"Gather up the fragments that remain, that nothing be lost."
—JOHN 6:12

Character Building Journal

1. In this chapter, you can see how Elsie learned about or applied the positive character trait of ORDERLINESS. In what areas of your life could you put this good character quality into practice? List some ideas in your Journal.

2. In what ways have you exemplified or shown to others this character quality? List them in your Journal.

3. Are there areas of your life that could use a little improvement with regard to ORDERLINESS? List those in your Journal as well and talk with your parents about ways for you to improve in this area.

PATIENCE

Accepting a difficult situation from God without giving Him a deadline to remove it.

Elsie Shows Patience with Arthur

Arthur was being his typical naughty self by teasing and bothering me at the most inopportune moments. I so wanted to work through my school problems, but he would not leave me alone. He began to tickle me on the back of the neck.

I tried to persuade him to leave me alone by telling him that I needed to work through school problems. He argued that he could have finished the problems over several times. I gave him a bit more information about how these two problems were not coming out right. He took interest and asked how I knew they were not right. I told him that I had the answer.

Arthur could not comprehend why I did not just set down the answer, if I had it. He pulled my hair a bit. I asked him not to pull my hair and then explained that simply setting down the answers would not be the honest thing to do.

> *"And not only so, but we glory in tribulation also: knowing that tribulation worketh patience."*
>
> —ROMANS 5:3

Elsie Uses Patience with Miss Stevens

Miss Stevens had bought some books for me as a gift and was so anxious to get close to me (I think in order to get close to Papa) that she suggested I sit right down in her room and read them.

Now I loved to read books, but I was not sure I would be allowed to read books that Miss Stevens gave me, unless I asked Papa first.

Miss Stevens was focused on the idea that I would look at, and therefore, receive her books, especially after I told her I could not eat the candy she had offered me. Both were very tempting for a young girl my age.

After she told me that she would be quite hurt if I wouldn't accept her books, I told her I would take them but would just look at the pictures until Papa had a chance to review their contents. I began to look over the pictures very slowly. Actually, I really did want to read the stories in the books, but I knew I would have to wait until Papa came to do this. I knew that Papa would not be home for a long time. Then Miss Stevens made the suggestion that she could read them and concluded it would be her reading them and not me.

I was shocked by her proposal and said, "Oh! No, ma'am, thank you, I know you mean to be kind, but I could not do it. It would be very wrong—quite the same, I am sure, as if I read it with my own eyes."

"But that on the good ground are they, which in an honest and good heart, having heard the word, keep it, and bring forth fruit with patience."

—LUKE 8:15

Other Character Traits Demonstrated

Though the books and the store-bought candy that Miss Stevens had offered certainly tempted Elsie a great deal, she showed plenty of SELF-CONTROL. She did not forget herself and what her Papa told her, which probably helped her not to succumb to something that she would have been sorry for later.

The Character of Elsie Dinsmore

"For I am full of matter, the spirit within me constraineth me."

—Job 32:18

Elsie tried very hard to use DISCRETION with Miss Stevens, who was determined to get her to accept something of which her Papa would not approve. Miss Stevens was one of those people who made it hard not to come right out and tell her that she was wrong, but discretion dictated that it may be best not to do so, mainly because one might fall into sin doing so.

"When thou sittest to eat with a ruler, consider diligently what is before thee."

—Proverbs 23:1

Character Building Journal

1. In this chapter, you can see how Elsie learned about or applied the positive character trait of PATIENCE. In what areas of your life could you put this good character quality into practice? List some ideas in your Journal.

2. In what ways have you exemplified or shown to others this character quality? List them in your Journal.

3. Are there areas of your life that could use a little improvement with regard to PATIENCE? List those in your Journal as well and talk with your parents about ways for you to improve in this area.

PUNCTUALITY

Showing high esteem for other people and their time.

Elsie Shows Punctuality to Miss Allison

One of the greatest pleasures I ever experienced was being granted the opportunity to read the Bible with my dear friend, Miss Rose Allison. She had a special understanding and love for God's Word. I learned a great deal from her during these times.

When Miss Allison said I could come at eight o'clock in the morning, the early hour did not bother me. Reading the Bible was more important to me than sleep. I also realized that it would be important to be respectful of Miss Allison's time. She always began reading at this hour so as to have two hours to read before joining the family circle.

Right at eight o'clock, I knocked softly at her door. I had gone down and picked some fresh roses as a special gesture to thank her for allowing me to join her. She opened the door expectantly and invited me in with open arms. She thanked me for the roses and called me darling.

I remember how she commented about my punctuality and showed a look of respectful appreciation for my consideration.

"To every thing there is a season, and a time to every purpose under the heaven."

—ECCLESIASTES 3:1

Character Building Journal

1. In this chapter, you can see how Elsie learned about or applied the positive character trait of PUNCTUALITY. In what areas

of your life could you put this good character quality into practice? List some ideas in your Journal.

    2.   In what ways have you exemplified or shown to others this character quality? List them in your Journal.

    3.   Are there areas of your life that could use a little improvement with regard to PUNCTUALITY? List those in your Journal as well and talk with your parents about ways for you to improve in this area.

RESPONSIBILITY

Knowing and doing what God and others are expecting of me.

Elsie Shows Arthur Her Responsibility

It was not uncommon for me to have to wrestle with Arthur while trying to finish my lessons at school. This always was the case when Miss Day left the room for a given time.

This day was not any different. Already, Arthur was pulling my hair, making many remarks, or twitching my book to try to distract me. He found great sport in trying to make me miserable and usually managed to accomplish it.

This morning, he could see that the blot on a page of my copy-book made me quite upset. He offered to tear out the page and fix it for me so Miss Day would not know the difference. However, I knew this would not be responsible, and I turned down his offer.

"Thank you, Arthur," I said, smiling through my tears. "You are very kind, but it would not be honest to do either, and I would rather stay at home than be deceitful."

"So then every one of us shall give account of himself to God."
—ROMANS 14:12

Related Character Trait

It is not too difficult to see VIRTUE in Elsie as she responded to her duty before God and others to do what is pure and morally excellent in this and other situations.

The Character of Elsie Dinsmore

"Finally, brothers, whatever is true, whatever is noble, whatever is right, whatever is pure, whatever is lovely, whatever is admirable— if anything is excellent or praiseworthy—think about such things."
—PHILIPPIANS 4:8, NIV

Elsie Shows Lucy Her Responsibility

Mrs. Carrington was seated with us at the dinner table, as were Lucy and Herbert. I looked at Herbert's pale face that remained from the strain he had suffered with a hip injury. I turned to ask him how his hip was. Herbert said it was better, and he didn't limp much now.

I was glad to hear that he had improved, but my cheerful attitude was the result of Papa being back with us again and seated with us at the table.

Miss Lucy was enjoying, or should I say indulging, in the meal. She had helped herself to the wonderful muffins that were set there. Before too long she turned her attention to me and asked me if I liked muffins.

I told her I liked them very much in a very cheerful tone. She seemed a bit baffled and then asked me why I was eating the cold bread and if I needed some butter on it. Then she summoned Pomp to pass me the butter.

"No, Lucy, I mustn't have it. Papa does not allow me to eat hot cakes or butter," I replied in the same cheerful voice.

"But to each one of us grace has been given as Christ apportioned it."
—EPHESIANS 4:7, NIV

Elsie Explains Her Responsibility to Miss Rose

Due to some circumstance with Harold and Sophy, I was late to tea one time. This played very heavily upon my conscience, since I knew that Papa would be vexed at me for not being there on time.

As a punishment, when I was offered the omelet and honey and cheese that were being served, I told Mrs. Allison, Rose's mother, that I would have to have dry bread for being late. I went on to explain that that is what Papa would want me to have.

Harold and then Sophy tired to defend me, saying it was not my fault I was late to tea. They even admitted that they had detained me. To this, Miss Rose said that I should go ahead and take the other food and that Papa would understand.

"You are very kind, Miss Rose, but you don't know my Papa as well as I do," I said a little sadly. "He told me I must always be in time to be ready for tea, and he says nothing excuses disobedience. You know, I could have come without the others. So I feel quite sure I would get nothing but bread for my supper if he were here."

I continued to hold this burden of responsibility in my heart through play and until my bedtime.

"Jesus said, 'If you were blind, you would not be guilty of sin; but now that you claim you can see, your guilt remains.'"
—JOHN 9:41, NIV

Other Character Traits Demonstrated

Elsie had acquired a strong reputation for her TRUTHFULNESS in small and large things alike. This case was no different. All were willing to acquit her and make no mention of it to her father. However, her responsibility to the One who is truth cancelled all excuses for her.

"These are the things that ye shall do; Speak ye every man the truth to his neighbour; execute the judgment of truth and peace in your gates."
—ZECHARIAH 8:16

Elsie showed SINCERITY about the gravity of her error. Her belief that she had done what was displeasing to Papa made her eager to do what was the right thing in her understanding of her Papa and his rules. She would not, therefore, eat anything but the cold, dry bread.

"Sanctify them through thy truth: thy word is truth."
—JOHN 17:17

Elsie demonstrated LOYALTY in her ability to show her commitment to God and to her Papa. She did not give up her commitment, though it brought her hardship—both spiritually and physically.

"Everyone must submit himself to the governing authorities,
for there is no authority except that which God has established.
The authorities that exist have been established by God."
—ROMANS 13:1, NIV

Character Building Journal

1. In this chapter, you can see how Elsie learned about or applied the positive character trait of RESPONSIBILITY. In what areas of your life could you put this good character quality into practice? List some ideas in your Journal.

2. In what ways have you exemplified or shown to others this character quality? List them in your Journal.

3. Are there areas of your life that could use a little improvement with regard to RESPONSIBILITY? List those in your Journal as well and talk with your parents about ways for you to improve in this area.

SECURITY

Structuring my life around that which is eternal and cannot be destroyed or taken away.

Elsie Shows Her Security to Papa

What a day for a trial this Sabbath day turned out to be, as we climbed into the carriage for what should have been a peaceful ride to church. Papa had bought a couple of young fiery steeds two days earlier, and Ajax harnessed them for the carriage ride.

The horses were so agitated that morning that Ajax seemed to use all his strength to hold them down. However, when Papa asked him about his ability to do so, Ajax stated that he had worked with the horses and had become familiar with them. He felt confident with his ability to expertly handle the team.

On the way to church, the young horses rejoiced with great exuberance and went on very briskly. It was as thrilling a ride as ever I had, and Papa was constantly on the look out, expecting something bad to happen any moment along the way. We did make it to church safely, but there had been some quick moments of doubt in Papa's mind that he attempted to keep to himself.

Things were a bit worse on the way home. The horses took fright on the way, and going downhill, they began to rush along at a furious rate. At this, I could see that Papa was frightened about what would become of us. He picked me up and set me down between his knees for protection.

When I looked up into his face, he looked pale, and his eyes were fixed upon me with an expression of anguish. "Dear Papa," I whispered, "God will take care of us."

The Character of Elsie Dinsmore

"Labour not for the meat which perisheth, but for that meat which endureth unto everlasting life, which the Son of man shall give unto you: for him hath God the Father sealed."

—JOHN 6:27

Related Character Trait

Elsie was as concerned for her Papa as her Papa was for her during the carriage incident. During this time, she was able to use SENSITIVITY to discern that her Papa was frightened and did not have the security that she had in God.

". . . and call upon me in the day of trouble; I will deliver you, and you will honor me."

—PSALM 50:15, NIV

Elsie Demonstrates Security in Darkness

I had planned to try to get up early that morning to be able to slip into Papa's room and set my gift to him on his table where he could see it. I really preferred for gifts to be surprises instead of presenting them straightforwardly. Somehow, it seemed so much more exciting.

It was good that I heard the clock strike five that morning. I carefully slipped from my bed and out into the dark hallway. All was darkness and silence in the house, but I had no thought of fear. I found Papa's door and was delighted to be able to place the package there without him waking.

"And he saith unto them, Why are ye fearful, O ye of little faith? Then he arose, and rebuked the winds and the sea; and there was a great calm."

—MATTHEW 8:26

Character Building Journal

1. In this chapter, you can see how Elsie learned about or applied the positive character trait of SECURITY. In what areas of your life could you put this good character quality into practice? List some ideas in your Journal.

2. In what ways have you exemplified or shown to others this character quality? List them in your Journal.

3. Are there areas of your life that could use a little improvement with regard to SECURITY? List those in your Journal as well and talk with your parents about ways for you to improve in this area.

SELF-CONTROL

Instant obedience to the initial prompting of God's Spirit.

Elsie Shows Self-Control with Papa

I found the need to call on God's strength almost every day while living at Roselands, for each hour brought on its own trial. No one but the servants, who loved me dearly, treated me with kindness. However, coldness and neglect were the least I had to bear.

I was constantly reminded, even by Walter and Enna, that I was stubborn and disobedient, which gave so little pleasure to my walks and rides, either when I took them alone or in company with them. So, I eventually decided it was best to give up these activities altogether.

Then, one day, Mrs. Dinsmore drew Papa's attention to the fact by saying that it was no wonder I was growing pale and thin, because I did not exercise enough to keep my health. Papa called me to him and severely reprimanded me. He demanded that I take a walk and ride every day, when the weather would at all permit, but I was not to dare go alone any farther than into the garden.

At this, I answered Papa with meek submission, promising obedience, and then I turned quickly away to hide the emotion that was swelling in my breast. It was very painful to see my father so bitter with me after he was so fond and indulgent up to that time. It seemed like the only time he took notice of me was to utter a rebuke of some kind.

"And they that are Christ's have crucified
the flesh with the affections and lusts.

If we live in the Spirit, let us also walk in the Spirit."
—GALATIANS 5:24-25

Other Character Traits Demonstrated

Elsie came to a period in her life where she was more committed than ever to what she knew God wanted her to do. He wanted her MEEKNESS to step ahead of any anger she would allow, and she knew this could only happen if she would give up her personal rights to Him and remain in submission to her Papa's commands.

"Truly my soul waiteth upon God: from him cometh my salvation."
—PSALM 62:1

Elsie had to wait on the Lord to work the trials she was made to endure to His good in her, and this took a lot of PATIENCE. God asked her, effectively, to wait for His time to do this and not demand that He do it by a deadline.

"And not only so, but we glory in tribulations also:
knowing that tribulation worketh patience and patience, experience;
and experience, hope."
—ROMANS 5:3-4

Elsie Demonstrates Self-Control

Papa had been punishing me for what he deemed willful disobedience, and in order to carry it out, he had seen fit to restrict a certain number of my privileges. I had been missing Miss Rose dearly for quite some time when Adelaide brought a letter to me that had arrived from her.

I explained to Aunt Adelaide that, though I desired to read the letter very much, I would have to ask Papa if it was all right that I receive it. We took the letter to Papa, and he told Aunt Adelaide to give the letter to him. He said that I would not be allowed to read the letter until I submitted my will wholly to him.

To have this letter denied me that I wanted now so very desperately was a great disappointment to me. I had a very hard struggle with myself before I could put away entirely my feelings of anger and impatience.

Then, I thought about it and realized that this was not honoring my Papa. He might have a good reason for doing this, and as I belonged to him, he certainly had a right to everything that is mine. So, I decided to be submissive and wait patiently until he saw fit to give me my letter.

"But put ye on the Lord Jesus Christ, and make not provision for the flesh, to fulfil the lusts thereof."
—ROMANS 13:14

Character Building Journal

1.   In this chapter, you can see how Elsie learned about or applied the positive character trait of SELF-CONTROL. In what areas of your life could you put this good character quality into practice? List some ideas in your Journal.

2.   In what ways have you exemplified or shown to others this character quality? List them in your Journal.

3.   Are there areas of your life that could use a little improvement with regard to SELF-CONTROL? List those in your Journal as well and talk with your parents about ways for you to improve in this area.

SINCERITY

Eagerness to do what is right with transparent motives.

Elsie Shows Sincerity before God

One afternoon after Papa came home, we were sitting around the table when he came into the room. Enna jumped up to greet Papa, threw her arms around his neck, and said, "Good morning, brother Horace. I want a kiss." He replied that she should have it and then proceeded to kiss her several times followed with some hugs.

Papa, referring to my fearing his anger at times, said to Enna so I could hear, "You are not afraid of me. Are you? Nor sorry that I have come home?"

"No, indeed," said Enna.

They both glanced across the room at me where my eyes were swelling with tears. I could not help feeling that Enna had my place within Papa's arms, receiving his affection. I could see by Papa's face that he was not pleased that I looked jealous and did not approve of it at all. I tried to hide my tears, but soon I had to run out of the room for I could not hold them back.

Then I had this sincere thought. I was jealous and envious of Enna. "How wicked," I thought to myself, and I prayed, "Dear Savior, help me! Please take away these sinful feelings."

"Seeing ye have purified your souls in obeying the truth through the Spirit unto unfeigned love of the brethren, see that ye love one another with a pure heart fervently."

—1 PETER 1:22

Related Character Trait

Elsie had to get some quick perspective from God's point. It took some WISDOM for a girl her age to figure out that her emotions were for the wrong reasons.

"The fear of the LORD is the beginning of wisdom: and the knowledge of the holy is understanding."

—PROVERBS 9:10

Elsie Shows Sincerity about Herself

Some people were coming by the house to see Papa one evening while we were at the table. I was quite disturbed at someone seeing me, because Papa had tied a handkerchief around my hand. I had accidentally let his rare bird go from beneath a vase. I mistakenly thought it was one of Arthur's cruel pranks. The thought of someone seeing me with my hand tied up so was quite embarrassing to me, and I was in tears over the idea. Papa said I was to remain seated with the handkerchief there, because he wanted to see remorse in me.

Papa, seeing that it really upset me, told me I must stop crying about such things and allowed me to go to my room. However, as I was leaving the room, he could see that I had something to say and asked for me to speak.

"I am very sorry I was naughty, Papa. Will you please forgive me?" I asked him this while speaking in a low voice and with a sob.

"Blessed is the man whose sin the LORD does not count against him and in whose spirit is no deceit."

—PSALM 32:2, NIV

Related Character Trait

Elsie showed her Papa RESPONSIBILITY by doing what he expected her to do, and she came to realize she needed to be obedient to him. Obedience is something God expected from her.

"The righteousness of the righteous man will be credited to him, and the wickedness of the wicked will be charged against him."
—EZEKIEL 18:20B, NIV

Character Building Journal

1. In this chapter, you can see how Elsie learned about or applied the positive character trait of SINCERITY. In what areas of your life could you put this good character quality into practice? List some ideas in your Journal.

2. In what ways have you exemplified or shown to others this character quality? List them in your Journal.

3. Are there areas of your life that could use a little improvement with regard to SINCERITY? List those in your Journal as well and talk with your parents about ways for you to improve in this area.

THRIFTINESS

Not letting myself or others spend that which is not necessary.

Elsie Uses Her Thriftiness with Arthur

Arthur was not very good at setting aside money from his allowance, and, at his own admission, it was not easy for him to have the money he needed for very long. This day he came to me for what he referred to as a loan until his next allowance.

I really did not expect him to pay me back, knowing that I had more than I ever had a chance to spend. I also realized that it really belonged to the Lord, and He allowed me to have it to show stewardship and kindness toward others in need.

When Arthur explained that he had seen a small ship that he wanted, my first thought was to draw out my purse and give him the money. Then I hesitated and put it back in my pocket, and Arthur was not happy that I put it away.

I had an idea that would keep him from spending the money incorrectly, or losing it. I thought it might be better if I bought the ship for him and surprised him. So, I pretended that I had to do some thinking about lending him a whole five dollars. I told him I would let him know by tomorrow.

"If therefore ye have not been faithful in the unrighteous mammon, who will commit to your trust the true riches?"

—LUKE 16:11

Related Character Trait

Elsie showed RESOURCEFULNESS in her ability to put the money to wise use, rather than allow Arthur to waste it on candy or gambling, which he later had a propensity to do.

"His lord said unto him, Well done, thou good and faithful servant: thou hast been faithful over a few things, I will make thee ruler over many things: enter thou into the joy of thy lord."

—MATTHEW 25:21

Character Building Journal

1. In this chapter, you can see how Elsie learned about or applied the positive character trait of THRIFTINESS. In what areas of your life could you put this good character quality into practice? List some ideas in your Journal.

2. In what ways have you exemplified or shown to others this character quality? List them in your Journal.

3. Are there areas of your life that could use a little improvement with regard to THRIFTINESS? List those in your Journal as well and talk with your parents about ways for you to improve in this area.

TRUTHFULNESS

Earning future trust by accurately reporting past facts.

Elsie Shows Truthfulness to Papa

I was with Herbert, Arthur, Walter, Jim, and Lucy up the road from our house one day when we were walking for exercise and talking about things. Herbert had his bow and arrows with him. We were tired, so we sat beside the road near the meadow to rest.

When I had finished telling a story I knew, Herbert remarked that he thought we were rested enough and took an arrow from his pack. He shot it into the air and over into the meadow, exclaimed how far it must have flown, and asked me to go get it for him.

I felt sorry about how Herbert could not move very quickly because of his hip. So, forgetting Papa's prohibition, I ran to get the arrow in the meadow. No sooner than I had done this, it came to my mind that I had broken Papa's command not to go into the meadow.

I was so upset that I started to run back to the house immediately. I was crying and could not even answer Herbert's query as to what was wrong. As I reached the yard, I asked the servant where Papa was. He told me he must be in the house.

When I reached Papa, he saw that I was upset and asked me if I were hurt or sick. "No, Papa, not either," I confessed. "But— but—Oh, Papa! I have been a very naughty girl. I disobeyed you, Papa. I—I have been in the meadow."

"Wherefore putting away lying, speak every man truth with his neighbor: for we are members one of another."

—EPHESIANS 4:25

Elsie Shows Her Truthfulness to Papa

Arthur got a bit mischievous, as he often did, and seeing Grandpa's watch dangling from the pocket of his coat, which was draped over a chair, he yielded to temptation and ran off to play with it. It was not very wise of him and turned out to be the wrong choice for Arthur and everyone else.

Arthur was climbing a tree with the watch when it fell from his hand and hit the ground, cracking the crystal and denting the case. Arthur threatened us all not to tell on him, and he nearly punched me when I said I would tell the truth if questioned about it.

The problem was that Arthur did not want to pay for his mistake and said he would tell Grandpa that Jim, the servant, took it if anyone asked him about the incident.

The time came that I had been dreading when Papa asked if I knew anything about it. I had to tell the truth, because I was defending Jim. I told Papa that I had been there and knew it was not Jim who had broken the watch. I did not want to tell who it was, but I did not want Jim to suffer for something he did not do, either.

Papa said that, if I knew anything about who did it, I must tell or Jim would be beaten and sent off to the plantation for hard labor. This would distress his mother exceedingly. I was convinced I must tell the truth and proceeded to do so, though reluctantly, in a straightforward manner.

> *"These are the things that ye shall do; Speak ye every man the truth to his neighbour; execute the judgment of truth and peace in your gates: and let none of you imagine evil in your hearts against his neighbour; and love no false oath: for all these are things that I hate, saith the LORD."*

—ZECHARIAH 8:16-17

Character Building Journal

1. In this chapter, you can see how Elsie learned about or applied the positive character trait of TRUTHFULNESS. In what areas of your life could you put this good character quality into practice? List some ideas in your Journal.

2. In what ways have you exemplified or shown to others this character quality? List them in your Journal.

3. Are there areas of your life that could use a little improvement with regard to TRUTHFULNESS? List those in your Journal as well and talk with your parents about ways for you to improve in this area.

VIRTUE

*The moral excellence and purity of spirit that radiate
from my life as I obey God's word.*

Elsie Shows Her Virtue to All

It almost pains me to remember the circumstance I am about
to describe. Papa was in the drawing room with Mrs. Dinsmore,
Aunt Adelaide, and some of his gentlemen friends when he began
something I wished he hadn't. He was proud of my musical ability and was saying how he would be glad to ask me down to play
for them.

Just as he went to pull the rope to ring the servant, Mrs.
Dinsmore cautioned him that he had better not. Papa asked her
why not. She said because it was Sunday, and I would not obey
him to play on the Sabbath. Mrs. Dinsmore knew, because she had
tried to get me to read fairy tales on the Sabbath and found me
stubborn about it.

Papa defiantly pulled for the servant and asked that I be
requested, growing sorry that he had, because he remembered my
scruples. He suddenly realized I would not do it. At any rate, he
still commanded me to sit down at the piano and play. And, of
course, I told him that I could not on the Sabbath.

The scene got worse after I told Papa with pleading eyes,
brimming full of tears, "Dear Papa, I cannot sing it today. I cannot
break the Sabbath."

*"And beside this, giving all diligence, add to your faith
virtue; and to virtue knowledge."*

—2 PETER 1:5

Other Character Traits Demonstrated

This predicament allowed Elsie to demonstrate her LOYALTY to God during one of the most difficult times in her life. She so wanted to be obedient always to her Papa but only when it was not something that was wrong in the eyes of God.

"I am crucified with Christ: nevertheless I live; yet not I, but Christ liveth in me: and the life which I now live in the flesh I live by the faith of the Son of God, who loved me, and gave himself for me."
—GALATIANS 2:20

There were some mental roadblocks or maybe stumbling blocks around which Elsie needed to try to guide her father and others. This was not easy, however. Elsie used her virtuous appeal to demonstrate PERSUASIVENESS to her Papa before the others.

"A bruised reed shall he not break, and the smoking flax shall he not quench: he shall bring forth judgment unto truth."
—ISAIAH 42:3

Character Building Journal

1. In this chapter, you can see how Elsie learned about or applied the positive character trait of VIRTUE. In what areas of your life could you put this good character quality into practice? List some ideas in your Journal.

2. In what ways have you exemplified or shown to others this character quality? List them in your Journal.

3. Are there areas of your life that could use a little improvement with regard to VIRTUE? List those in your Journal as well and talk with your parents about ways for you to improve in this area.

WISDOM

Seeing and responding to life's situations from God's frame of reference.

Elsie Shows Wisdom before God

After Papa sent Mammy away, Adelaide was with me for awhile and then left me. I was quite alone, and even though Aunt Adelaide tried to reassure me, I knew somehow that Papa was going to punish me by sending me to a place like a convent and that they would make me renounce my faith in Jesus alone. I just knew in my heart that I would not be allowed to see my Papa again.

When I was left alone, I fell on my knees in earnest prayer, weeping and sobbing. It seemed like much more than I could bear. Then I thought of Christ's agony in the garden and His bitter cry, "Father, if it be possible, let this cup pass from me!" followed by His submissive prayer, "If this cup may not pass from me except I drink it, thy will, not mine, be done."

After this thought, I opened my Bible and read of His great sufferings, so meekly and patiently borne, without a single murmur or complaint. These sufferings had been borne by the One who was free from all stain of sin and borne not for Himself, but for others—sufferings to which my own were not for a moment to be compared. Then I prayed that I might bear the image of Jesus and that, like Him, I might be able to yield a perfect submission to my heavenly Father's will and to endure with patience and meekness whatever trial He might see fit to appoint me.

"The fear of the LORD is the beginning of wisdom: and the knowledge of the holy is understanding."
—PROVERBS 9:10

Other Character Traits Demonstrated

Elsie, understanding the Lord's desire to follow His heavenly Father's will even in His hour of sorrow in the garden, knew in her MEEKNESS that she must begin to yield her personal rights and expectations to God. Much like Jesus, it was not something simple for her to do.

"It is better to trust in the LORD than to put confidence in man."
—PSALM 118:8

Though Elsie, being very young, desired that this hard time of trial for her be over quickly, she showed PATIENCE toward God by not making demands that He end it. She accepted His timing, bearing much pain, and did not give Him a deadline of any kind.

"And he said unto me, My grace is sufficient for thee:
for my strength is made perfect in weakness. Most gladly
therefore will I rather glory in my infirmities, that the power of
Christ may rest upon me. Therefore I take pleasure in infirmities,
in reproaches, in necessities, in persecutions, in distresses for
Christ's sake: for when I am weak, then am I strong."
—2 CORINTHIANS 12:9-10

Character Building Journal

1. In this chapter, you can see how Elsie learned about or applied the positive character trait of WISDOM. In what areas of your life could you put this good character quality into practice? List some ideas in your Journal.

2. In what ways have you exemplified or shown to others this character quality? List them in your Journal.

3. Are there areas of your life that could use a little improvement with regard to WISDOM? List those in your Journal as well and talk with your parents about ways for you to improve in this area.

EPILOGUE

It is our hope that this book has brought delight to your heart and benefited you in your daily walk with the Lord. We have attempted to use Martha Finley's character, Elsie Dinsmore, to demonstrate how it is truly possible for someone who is dedicated to the Lord to walk with Him. We all share in one common malady, which is summed up as our sin. That sin amounts to the failure to trust, as Elsie learned to do, in Jesus Christ alone. God is sovereign in every way, and we can learn from sweet little Elsie how reliance on Him can bring comfort in the storms of our daily lives. We also can see through her experience how the pressure put on us by God-given authorities can test the metal of which we are made, refining our impurities and making us holy and ready for Him. As we grow with Elsie in the Lord, let us shine our light before men that in seeing good things that we do, they give glory to God. That God may richly bless you is our continual prayer.

THE ORIGINAL ELSIE CLASSICS

Elsie Dinsmore
Elsie's Holidays at Roselands
Elsie's Girlhood
Elsie's Womanhood
Elsie's Motherhood
Elsie's Children
Elsie's Widowhood
Grandmother Elsie
Elsie's New Relations
Elsie at Nantucket
The Two Elsies
Elsie's Kith and Kin
Elsie's Friends at Woodburn
Christmas with Grandma Elsie
Elsie and the Raymonds
Elsie Yachting with the Raymonds
Elsie's Vacation
Elsie at Viamede
Elsie at Ion
Elsie at the World's Fair
Elsie's Journey on Inland Waters
Elsie at Home
Elsie on the Hudson
Elsie in the South
Elsie's Young Folks
Elsie's Winter Trip
Elsie and Her Loved Ones
Elsie and Her Namesakes

Index of Scripture Texts

Index of Scripture Texts

Index of Character Traits